IN THE GAME OF DECE

# UNDISCLOSED
### A TALE OF LOVE AND DECEIT

# DEIIRA SMITH-COLLARD

# UNDISCLOSED
## A TALE OF LOVE AND DECEIT

A Novel

By

DeiIra Smith-Collard

**ISBN-13: 978-0-9818132-2-6**

Cover Design by
Depictions of Life Photography & Design

AriSiri Publishing
340 N. Sam Houston Pkwy E
Houston, TX 77060
Printed in the U.S.A

# DEDICATION

This novel is dedicated to all the beautiful women who had the odds stacked against them, but never counted themselves out.
These are the women who dive deep inside of themselves to find their light and shine brighter than people ever thought possible.

Keep shining!

# ACKNOWLEDGMENTS

I feel so honored and humbled as I'm writing my acknowledgements. For so long I thought I lost my voice and my desire to write. There were a million stories inside of me, screaming to get out but I was somehow, broken. Then one day I realized I had a God given gift and talent to create. I began writing and didn't stop. Now, I'm back and better than ever.

To my wonderful family, thank you for your endless support and encouragement.

Dana Pittman, thank you so much for motivating me and believing in me enough to light that fire under me. You push me to be a better writer, I'm in awe of your expertise.

Josie Sloan, thank you so much for always being here for me. I am blessed to have a friend like you. A friend that will rock with you through thick and thin, and who truly wants nothing better than the best for you.

To Lulu Botello, my fearless fuego warrior. You are bigger than life and inspire me everyday. Thank you for being a voice of honesty in my writing process and a constant motivation.

Lastly, but most importantly thank you to my readers. You all make this possible, without loyal readers my voice goes unheard. Thank you for the endless support. Enjoy this just as you did the last and the many more to come.

# PROLOGUE

*Yo ass got til Friday to get
the hell out of this state!
Get out or find your home in
one of these bayous!
I'll feed yo ass to the gators
and they will never find you
You been warned!*

The sudden attack of the words jolted my heart and left me in a state of disbelief. This was not at all how I expected my Thursday to go. Every nerve ending within my body exploded with infuriating heat, engulfing me in anger. Now part of me wanted to wait it out and dare a bitch to come at me. That was the real in me talking, but the smart me said there was someone just as real out there; waiting to prove her point. The thud of the door hitting the wall as I entered my home echoed my emotions. I slammed the door shut and threw my bags against the sofa.

"Think Dominique, think girl!" With the speed of a sprinter, my mind raced to create a plan. Staring at the white piece of notebook paper I found on my door I knew it was from a woman and most likely it was from my man's wife. I say my man cause he took care of me, he paid for this house, kept my pockets full and made sure I had nothing but the best. It didn't matter to me that he had a wife at home, his wife wasn't my problem, it was his.

At least that's what I thought. For years I knew this woman existed, but again, she wasn't my problem. Until now, now his pain in the ass wife was making a formal introduction and I heard her loud and clear. Had I met Queen under different circumstances we may have been cool, we shared much of the same taste, especially when it came to men.

I always knew who Queen was, everyone did and I had even met her a couple of times, but she just thought I was on Redd's payroll. She didn't know I was the main side chick dipping into the pockets she thought belonged to her.

My footsteps created a path of dismay as I walked the length of the room. Shit! What was I going to do? My heels clicked against the mahogany colored wood as I marched from one end of the living room to the other. I stood still for a moment, taking in my surroundings. My apartment was everything a girl like me could hope for. From the muted steel colored upholstery to the pops of purple throughout the room, it was all me.

I didn't want to leave it, but if it was Queen who sent me the threat, I knew she had the means and the power to follow through. I mean, she had the whole hood backing her. Queen had been with Redd since high school and I knew when it came down to it she had a team waiting to get a piece of me just cause she had told them to.

Some of these bitches were so thirsty to be in her presence they would kill on command. Redd and Queen were hood royalty and every nothing ass nigga and dusty hood bitch was dying to be in their court.

I've never been a stupid woman and I didn't plan on starting now. I made up my mind at that very moment. No use staying so that I could prove I wasn't scared. I would be lying to myself anyway. I walked to the back of my apartment and moved the picture in front of the large wall safe that Redd used to stash his valuables.

He had it installed right after I moved in. I agreed to stash the cash here and he agreed, I just wasn't allowed to know the combination. Or so his dumb ass thought. Anytime he opened it he made me turn my back or leave the room. What the dummy didn't know is when I turned my back; I faced a mirror and saw his every move.

"2-10-5-7," I said the combination aloud as I turned the dial. My fingers trembled, Redd had a key to this apartment and came and went as he pleased. I didn't expect him, but I never knew what to expect from him. I glanced towards the door and dashed towards it to bolt the top lock. At least that way I would hear him unlocking both locks and give myself a little extra time to hide what I was doing.

Once I made it back to the safe, I eased the door open and saw stacks and stacks of cash. I don't know exactly how much was in this safe. All I saw was racks on racks on racks, it was enough cash to get me the hell out of the state of Louisiana and some place better, some place where I knew I could be safe. I stuffed the money into the biggest purse I could find and closed it. Taking only the clothes on my back, I got in my car and drove straight down I-10 until I arrived in Houston, TX.

This is the place I will start over, this is where Dominique Simoneaux will re-invent herself.

# CHAPTER 1

S itting at the dinner table next to my husband I admired him, he was truly handsome. The light from the dimly lit reception hall bounced off his smooth ebony skin, landing on his chiseled chin and full lips. After twelve years of marriage, we still had a passion that burned hotter than any fire. I knew how to be the lighter to his fuse, and I would always be here to support anything that would lead him to greatness. We were yet again at another benefit his firm was sponsoring.

I don't know if we were feeding the homeless, clothing the children or donating blood, his company was always trying to save the world and I could barely keep up with which cause they were fighting for.

I smiled and interacted like a good little lawyer's wife. Trent was a partner at one of the largest firms in Houston. He had broken through the barriers and was one of the few African American men employed by Smith, Masters & Jamison. We were the Jamison part. Boredom was creeping in while listening to the many speeches and bad jokes. I leaned into my husband and excused myself.

"Baby, please excuse me," I leaned into my

husband and I whispered in his ear.

"Where you off to Kyra?" Trent's mouth spread into the million dollar smile that helped him acquit guilty people every day.

"The ladies room." Smiling, I slowly pushed my seat away from the table to stand. The black evening gown I wore clung snuggly to my hips. With my body swaying to the music that played in the background, I made my way to the restroom. Pushing the heavy door open, I walked in and quickly surveyed the stalls.

"Whew, I'm alone."

I needed the quietness this restroom offered. My back landed against the wall as I deeply inhaled the floral aroma of lavender and jasmine and then exhaled all of the exhaustive tension that resided in the pit of my stomach. My eyes roamed the room, taking in the nice decor. The restroom was decorated like a small sitting room with plush sofas and oversized chairs where one could wait in comfort.

No long lines would form outside of these doors. The marble countertops sparkled as if they had been newly polished, glistening in the warm recessed lighting that made them seem to glow.

The door opening interrupted my contemplation of the countertops. I moved closer to the sink to allow the woman entrance and to limit any unnecessary interaction. The woman's smile seemed to be carved into her creamy skin. It struck a chord of familiarity with me.

Trying not to stare I fumbled through my purse to find my lipstick and compact. I dabbed the sponge against my face to refresh my makeup. Through the reflection in the mirror, I could see her eyes on me. For an unusually long time, her eyes drifted over my features. Without taking my eyes off of her I snapped the small black case closed. What the hell did she want?

"I use MAC too, it's awesome isn't it?" Her voice sang the sweet song of a Louisiana native.

"Yes, it is." I smiled and continued to mind my business. My interest in her conversation was only surface deep, I would prefer not to be bothered and surely she couldn't have stared me down that long just to tell me she likes the makeup I use.

"I believe I know you." She tightened the space between us and was now far too close for my comfort. My deep breaths and exaggerated sighs should have been signs of my budding annoyance. Didn't she come in here to use the restroom? I was curious as to why she hadn't done so.

"I don't think so," I responded with a smile

and began to place my cosmetics back into my bag. I watched in the mirror as her eyes burned deep holes into the side of my face.

"Yeah, Yeaaah, I know you, your name is Dominique, Dominique Simoneaux, am I right?" It was more of a statement than a question. I finally turned to face the woman.

I laughed, "I think we have a case of mistaken identity. Let me introduce myself," I extended my right hand to her. "My name is Kyra Jamison, and you are?" She reached to shake my hand. I noticed her immaculate French manicure and diamond rings she wore, pricey diamonds.

"You can call me Queen." I sensed a bit of sarcasm in her voice. She spoke as if I already knew her name. Her eyes were on fire, ignited with anger. She looked at me as if she attempted to look through me.

"Queen, that's very unique. Well, I am pleased to meet you. I have to excuse myself though, my husband will be giving a speech shortly, it was nice talking with you."

Hurriedly, I exited the restroom. Something about this woman made me uneasy and I was more than happy to excuse myself from her presence. I practically ran back to my table and the comfort of the familiar faces. Just as I was about to take my seat I heard that voice behind me.

"Dominique, you forgot your purse." I turned to receive the small Dior bag I was carrying.

"It's Kyra, and thank you very much for bringing this to me. I do appreciate it." With one swift motion, I collected my purse from her and turned to take my seat. This was her cue to walk away from the table. My purse was returned, her presence was no longer needed but instead, I watched as she grabbed the nearest empty chair and invited herself to the table.

"Mr. Jamison," She spoke. "How are you?" Trent looked at her as if she were an alien. I could tell he did not recognize her. Her head flew back as she released a boisterous laugh. "I work as a paralegal in your firm. You know, I'm assigned to most of your cases."

A spark of recognition flickered in my husband's eyes. "Queen, great to see you. I hardly recognized you without your glasses and your hair down. How are you this evening?"

"Well, that's the power of contacts and a flat iron." Again her loud laugh echoed through the room. For reasons unknown to me, I didn't like her. Her shifty eyes and knowing stares made me uneasy but it seemed that I was the only one to notice them. I didn't participate much in the conversation because her mindless chit-chat and country grammar reminded me of times I didn't care to think of.

"Sweetie, Queen relocated to Houston after Hurricane Katrina."

"So, how long ago was that again?" Why would I care when and how she got here? I smiled but honestly didn't care. I could tell my husband was trying to engage me in the conversation. He wanted his forever entertaining wife to emerge.

I knew she wouldn't be making a debut as long as that woman sat at the table. I nodded and mumbled various things to entertain my husband's pleading eyes, but I was lost in my own thoughts.

The cadence of her voice held me captive as I gazed at her. The only thing that kept me from screaming at the top of my lungs was the hundreds of people in this room. Watching this woman was like watching a train wreck. You want to look away but you can't. Her energy intoxicated the table. She seduced them all with just her presence.

I sank back into the plush cushion of my chair and watched as they clung to her every word. My friends hungrily waited to devour her, greedy for more of her witty conversation. It was obvious that her beauty had captured them all. From the corner of my eye, I watched her every move.

It was easy to see how she had captivated the table, she was beautiful. Her smooth cappuccino colored skin and bright smile could fool anyone. Those almond-shaped amber eyes were incredibly innocent, but I knew different. Those same innocent doe-like eyes threw daggers at me when no one was looking. Between smiles, she would glance at me and wink with perceptive eyes. What was it that she thought she knew?

My stomach did summersaults as I watched her toss her long brown tresses and bat her lengthy Covergirl eyelashes. The night was finally nearing an end and I was ecstatic. I wanted to jump for joy as we walked towards our car.

"Would you and your date like to join us for drinks at our home Queen? A few of us from the firm are going to retire and have a few drinks, a little after party if you will." My husband could be very persuasive with just a smile.

"Now how could I say no to the boss." Queen stepped away from us long enough to call her date over. The one she had abandoned while she sat at my table. They moved towards us for what I assumed would be more introductions.

"This is my husband Lawrence." We all took turns shaking Lawrence's hand. I shuffled further and further back. I wanted to disappear. Lawrence's eyes locked with mine as he extended his hand towards me. I had to drive myself to touch him. His grasp was frigid and cold, almost as cold as his smile.

"How beautiful" The words slipped secretly from his lips, only audible to me. I noticed the Chinese letters tattooed along the side of his neck. Under the Chinese letters was one simple word in all caps, Redd. I snatched my hand back and retreated into the safety of my husband's shadow. Lawrence towered over me, his tall slender stature intimidating me. I trembled from the strength of his stare.

His piercing eyes wandered over my body slowly as if he was memorizing every inch of my curves. I searched for any and every reason to avoid eye contact with them. Every nerve ending my body possessed tingled with terror. I had to figure out of how to get out this situation.

I began to walk towards the car and opened the door to get in. I would normally wait for my husband but they made me anxious. My retreat to the car placed needed distance between us. I exhaled as my body sank into the plush leather seats. Resting my head on the headrest, my husband's pearl white Maserati became my refuge.

There were no roaming eyes or knowing stares in this car, I was finally alone. I shifted in my seat to see if I could spot how close they were in the rearview mirror. They were approaching. I knew I wasn't going to be able to play hostess tonight and the only way I could get out of it would be to fake a headache.

I know he hated when I seemed uninviting and I tried to keep him happy, but he was so worried about appearances. The car door opening was the finger snap I needed to bring me out of my trance.

"Kyra, why did you leave like that?" His smooth harmonious voice was concerned. He patiently waited for my answer but his eyes were consumed with worry.

"I have a headache baby." My voice was low, weak, and begging not to be questioned. This answer seemed to be enough because he never said another word. With every minute that passed, we came closer and closer to our home. The closer we got the more nervous I seemed to become. I didn't want these people in my house. I didn't know them and whatever they seem to have against me could only seem to get worse with inviting them into my personal space. I sat motionless as the car pulled into the three car garage. I almost forgot to breathe.

"Kyra, we're home." I heard his unspoken question, why hadn't I moved. I pushed the door open and stepped out. The mindless chatter in the background of the intruding lady, Queen floated through the garage, getting increasingly louder the closer she got.

Her voice carried through the hollow garage and with it traveled a pending disaster. I couldn't say why I felt this way, but it was something about the spark she carried in her eyes. I noticed it from the moment I saw her, her eyes said she was a woman with a vendetta, and vengeance would soon be hers.

Everyone talked while sipping midnight cocktails. Music played as the party started to really pick up. Any other night I would be right next to my husband, having a hell of a good time but tonight was different. Tonight I couldn't seem to pull it together.

All night I've felt both Queen and her husband threw glances with hidden messages, and somehow I was supposed to know what it was they meant. I was done with their cat and mouse game. I placed my hand on Trent's knee and leaned towards Trent. His facial hair brushed against my lips as I planted a kiss on his cheek.

"Baby, I think I'm going to go lay down. This headache is getting worse and worse, I'm going to take something and go to sleep." I was in no mood for a party. I finished my theatrics hoping he fell for this fake ache.

"Can't you stay a little while?" I looked regretfully as Trent gave me the sad puppy dog look.

"Baby, I-" He interrupted my sentence with a motion of his hand.

"I understand, I hope you feel better." He

gently kissed my hand as he led me to the long hallway that ended in the master bedroom. I couldn't close the door fast enough as I entered the room to finally find the peace I had been searching for all night.

I slid the straps of my sequined gown off of my shoulders and stepped out of it as it slipped off of my body and onto the floor. There was a low knock at the door. I wondered what Trent wanted. It was unlike him to leave a room full of guests. He was always the ever entertaining, always hospitable host. It must be important.

I walked to the double wooden bedroom doors, turned the lock and walked back to my dressing area without even turning around to greet him. Just as I reached for my robe, he spoke.

"Still just as beautiful as you have always been." The unfamiliar voice echoed throughout the large room. I turned to face the stranger.

"What are you doing in my room? You need to leave. Now!" How dare he just stroll into my room and watch me as I undress. That was beyond rude, it was repulsive.

"It's nothing I ain't never seen before."

"Leave, damn it." I felt like a small child in the company of a scary stranger. He cautiously moved towards me as his eyes began to dance over my body.

"Ohhh going back to our roots are we, I don't hear little miss proper no more, I hear Dominique from New Orleans, the one that grew up in the hood." His lips curled into a sinister smile. "Where you been hiding all night girl? Now that's the person I remember."

An uncomfortable silence stood between us. My heart pounded, pumping five times faster than normal as I stood motionless, scared to even allow my self to swallow.

"You really have cleaned up nice. I see how you live, fancy cars, million dollar homes, diamonds for every day of the week; tell me Dominique, did my money help you get here? You know the money you stole from me. I never forget a debt. No matter how long it's been, and thirteen years still ain't long enough for me to forget 500,000 dollars. Baby, that's half a mil and right about now I'm needing that plus some interest." He stopped talking only long enough to take a breath, then he moved closer to me.

I held my robe in front of my body attempting to cover myself. I was naked and I didn't want to be bare in front of this man. The silky threads slipped from my hands as he snatched my robe away from me exposing my body. I could feel the cold air caress my nipples as they began to become alert from the chill. He mistook this as an invitation. Lawrence's hand gently stroked my breast. I slapped his hand away.

"Get the hell out of my room, I'm not going to tell you or your crazy ass wife again, I'm not who you think I am, my name is Kyra, not Dominique!"

His eyes were full of determination and that determination seemed to be fueled by anger. With the quickness of a cheetah, he grabbed my neck and pushed me against the wall. His nails dug into my skin as he rendered me immobile by placing all his body weight on me. He was so close I could feel his erection press against me. The more pain he seemed to inflict the more excited he seemed to become. His hot breath burned against my skin as he moved close enough to whisper in my ear.

"Bitch, stop playing with me, I know you, from the curve of your hips to the scent of your pussy. Your hiding days are over, it's payback time." With the end of his speech, he released me. My body tumbled to the floor as I struggled to catch my breath. A minute longer and I'm sure I would have passed out. My heart was racing. Gazing up at this man he appeared larger than life. I shrank back into the corner, I wanted away from him. He glared at me and then just as quickly as he came, he was gone.

-

***

*Within the next six hours, I was in Houston, Texas. The big city left me in awe. I didn't have any relatives here so I was all alone. The first night I spent sleeping in my car and that became old fast, besides I didn't need to. I knew any motel I landed at wouldn't ask questions. I had been here for a week, ducking and dodging like the law was after me. Hell Redd was worse than the law and if he ever caught me I would be dead.*

*I needed to come up with a plan. I had way too much cash on me and had to find a place to stash it and a place to stay. I ended up someplace off I-45S. I didn't know what type of neighborhood this was, but I also didn't care. As long as I was around people that didn't know who the hell I was.*

*I grabbed the boxed hair dye I purchased from the first beauty supply store I could find. Not wanting my curly locks to fall out, I read the directions repeatedly. Once I felt confident I wouldn't mess it up I applied the kit and allowed it to work its magic.*

*I squeezed the towel to remove the excess water from my head and stared at my reflection. My hair had been transformed from its natural sandy brown color to jet black. It was different but I needed more. I grabbed the gray handled scissors I purchased and began to snip away at my hair.*

*I cut it in bold layers the best I could and used the bottle of Hawaiian Tropic to make my skin three shades darker than my normal caramel colored complexion. Granted it wasn't a total transformation but I did look different.*

*After days of listening and taking in my surroundings, I learned next door neighbor had the hookup. He sounded like someone I definitely needed to see. I needed a way to get myself established in a new city as a new person. I walked to his apartment.*

*"Hey Berto, what's up." His name was Humberto but everyone called him Berto for short.*

*"What's up, Mami?" He looked at me with raised eyebrows, waiting for me to state my case.*

*"Yeah, I heard you the guy to come to if I need things," I stressed the word things. He knew what was up so no sense in saying what I really came for. Basically, Berto and his brother Andres are the people you see when you need to get legal. I was legal, but my legal name would get me killed so I needed a new one. I started to open my mouth to explain, but before I could get a sentence out, Berto interrupted me. It was like he was reading my mind.*

*"Mami, I don't need your explanation. Keep it to ya self, as long as you payin' we can do bizness." He said. That was cool with me, the less people knew about Dominique Simoneaux the better.*

*"Cool, I will also need a degree in something like business or finance in that package. It needs to look good on my resume and if you know someone who could verify the info that would be even better."*

*"Yeah, I got you, you just have the money, a fifteen thousand for the first package, five thousand for the degree. I have it for you in two weeks." With that said, he snapped a picture of me and then I was dismissed and on to the next person.*

*True to his word, my package was ready for me two weeks later. I happily paid him from my stash of money careful not to let him see just how much I had. Once he left I went through the contents of the package. Damn, he was good cause this shit looked legal.*

*I had a new Texas issued driver's license, a social security card, credit cards in my new name, a Master's Degree in Finance, and a bomb ass resume with references and everything. Dominque has officially disappeared, it's time to do things a little different and Kyra Williams definitely knows how to live.*

# CHAPTER 2

Sleep evaded me the entire night. I begged for its comfort, even solicited help from Ambian but my nerves were too bad. Fear had battled fatigue and won. I had a delusional couple insisting I was this Dominique and I didn't know what to do. I laid in the bed staring silently at the ceiling until the promising signs of daylight crept through my window.

If I couldn't get rest perhaps I could relax by taking a warm shower. I delicately shifted the comfy covers from my body and planted my feet into the plush carpet. The bed moved as got up, I looked over my shoulder to make sure I hadn't awakened my husband. Trent was sleeping peacefully, ignorant to all the turmoil I was facing.

As soapy suds slid down my body I weighed my options. I was so consumed with my own thoughts that I didn't hear Trent when he walked through the door. He moved groggily through the bathroom as I eyed him through the frosted glass shower door. I couldn't help but think to my self how well I had done. His physique was like a work of art; each muscle chiseled to perfection. Thanks to an hour at the gym every day before work, his stomach was firm, with a well defined six pack. For my husband, appearance was everything.

My eyes roamed the length of his body stopping only when my gaze met his, we were both watching each other. A feeling I hadn't felt in years washed over me. It was like fire. It was the heated, searing passion that burned hot in the beginning of our marriage, but the years had made us complacent. I was praying he would surprise me by being spontaneous and divert my attention from its unwavering hold on my situation.

He stepped into the shower with me and pressed his lips against mine. Our tongues moved in unison as he pulled my body close to him. This was out of the ordinary for him. Trent had a routine he followed religiously, and his day couldn't start if anything was out of order.

Our kiss was deep and passionate. He hungrily explored every inch of my lips, neck and then body. His hands eagerly probed my body, excitedly trying to take in every inch of me. He held me tightly, so tight you would have thought he believed I would disappear. We kissed the way we did when we first met, before all the fancy cars and diamond rings. When he was fresh out of law school and I was a branch manager for Wells Fargo. This reminded me of the young passion that he once showed me.

Trent held my hands above my head and kissed me lightly on my breast. The suds still rolled down my legs as I began to get weak from the intensity of his kisses. The water danced erotically on our skin as he pressed himself against me. I could tell he wanted more. Unexpectedly, he grabbed me by my hips and turned me around so that now my back was to him.

He clasped my hands and held them behind my back as I became his prisoner, his hands my cuffs. Slowly he entered me. Each thrust was long, deep. Our bodies were close, touching as he moved inside of me. The water splashed against my hair and back, the warm fluid flowing over us, mixing with our perspiration of lust. He became more intense, moving faster, thrusting harder. I couldn't help calling out his name.

"Trent, baby, you feel so good" I needed more of him.

"You like it rough don't you? Take it, can you take all of me baby?" He began to thrust harder, whispering to me how good I felt, how deep he was, and how he was determined to make me cum. He pulled my hair, causing my head to tilt back against his chest. As if on cue, we both reached our orgasm.

"It's going to be hard to say goodbye to you." I thought I heard Trent whisper in my ear. I quickly dismissed it, too exhausted to decipher his jumbled jargon. I had no words to speak. My body was weak with ecstasy, and for a moment in time, I forgot my problems. I stood frozen, staring at the man who had changed my life. Just as quickly as he had come into the bedroom, he was gone.

Once I heard the click of the door shutting, I turned to the mirror and inhaled deeply. As soon as my moment with Trent was done, all of my problems came rushing back. Surveying my reflection in the mirror, I dried my jet black hair and parted it so that the long layers framed my face. It rested delicately on my shoulders as I used my flat iron to gently bend the ends.

The corners of my eyes curved upward as I smiled at myself, content with the woman that stared back at me. The light above the mirror danced across my eyes and reflected a vibrant chestnut brown color with a tiny hint of hazel. My eyebrows were arched to perfection and my luscious lips would give any of the Kardashians injected lips a run for their money. Once I finished styling my hair I began to dress for my date with the Galleria, if nothing else I needed to get out of the house and keep busy.

I parked my car and walked towards the mall. I still hadn't figured out what to do. The garage looked empty for a Friday afternoon. My steps echoed as I walked to the entrance. I heard movement behind me. I turned around expecting to see someone but there was nothing there. I continued to my destination attempting to shake the feeling of being stalked.

From store to store, I purchased any and everything I felt I wanted. Shopping seemed to always take my mind off whatever was bothering me and the fact that I was surrounded by thousands of people also gave me comfort.

I could get lost in the crowd. I left the mall with bags in hand. Hours and hours of endless spending had taken its toll on me; hopefully, I could go home and sleep. I walked into the dimly lit garage. Even though it was daylight, the air was hazy and it appeared to be much later than it actually was.

The massive structure surrounded me making me feel small and completely alone. I had made a poor choice parking so far away and in a corner. I should have just valeted. Uneasiness fueled my steps as I raced to the safety of my car. I unlocked the door and breathed a sigh of relief, then strapped myself in behind the wheel. The sound of the engine starting brought calm to my racing heart. I checked my rearview mirror before shifting the car into reverse.

"What the fuck?" I squinted to get a better look at the black figure that eyed me through the tiny mirror. I didn't know who or what the hell that was staring back at me, but I knew one thing I would fight like hell. I searched for something, anything to defend myself but before I could turn around I felt a slender arm seize my neck. I was rendered immobile as I felt the deathly embrace squeeze tighter.

The arm slinked around my neck like a serpent to its prey. The more I struggled, the firmer the grip. I pulled forward attempting to break free, but the more I pulled the stronger the grip became. I couldn't see my abductor but I could feel the warmth of angry frenzied breaths on the back of my neck.

"Remember the note, bitch? I meant it then and I mean it now. There are plenty of bayous in Texas you can find yourself in." Queen. Without releasing her grip the slightest bit, I felt her reach to my left and unlock the door. The passenger door flew opened and he slipped into the seat beside me.

"Hey there little lady, whatcha lookin' scared for?" I cut my eyes towards the man sitting next to me. His lips curled into a hateful scowl, and his eyes reflected the sentiment.

"Because I've told you I'm not who you think I am." My voice was muffled and distorted because of the lack of sufficient air.

"Bullshit." She spat as she squeezed my neck. Every time she spoke her hold on me became tighter. I struggled to breathe.

At this point, I began to weigh my options and it was evident I didn't have many. I would continue to be terrorized by this couple. I thought if I stuck to my guns, maybe they would believe they actually had a case of mistaken identity. I don't exactly look the same as I did then. I've lost weight, tanned my skin, changed my hair, and had worked hard to get rid of my native New Orleans accent.

The way I speak and interact with people is different, but somehow they had found me. They saw through my disguise and even though I made certain to cover my tracks, I obviously didn't dig a deep enough hole to bury my secret. From the corner of my eye, I could see Redd's menacing stare.

"Damn it, Redd, why can't you just leave me alone? The money I took was owed to me, yeah you paid my bills and put change in my pocket but that's all you did. Then this wife of yours threatened to kill me, what choice did I have?" I was shedding my mask. Dominique had surfaced.

"Finally she admits it." His cold hard stare made the tiny hairs on the nape of my neck stand at attention. Tiny prickles of panic coursed the length of my spine as I waited for him to finish. "I should kill you now, but dead men don't pay." My eyes widened as the sound of his laughter floated through the air. None of this shit was funny, he was talking about my life.

"I don't have anything to pay you." Queen still held me by my neck and I was unable to move.

"Come on now girl, don't insult me. I know you holdin' somethin'. I've been to your house. I know how you livin'."

"I don't make the money my husband does. I can move about 250,000 without it being noticed. I have to move it gradually, so he doesn't know, but that's all I got. It's been twelve years and I had to use that money to get on my feet."

Trent and I had a joint account, most of our money went into one account and there was no way in hell I could move that type of money without Trent or the bank realizing it. Trent would flip if a few hundred dollars were out of place, I could only imagine he would lose his shit over $500,000. This was the only way I could keep my life from falling apart. They would just have to take payments.

"That's all you got? What you mean that's all you got? You take all the money I stashed in that apartment and then the police raid me and put me out of business and before I could get back on my feet and get my business running again, that bitch hurricane Katrina came through and ran my ass out of the only place I called home.

Now you want to sit in your expensive ass car and tell me that's all you got. Hell naw, I need everything you took from me plus some interest. Listen you get me my money or I go tell your new sugar daddy just who you really are." He scowled.

"No! You can't do that!"

"Yes, I can, and I will unless you get me my money. You got one week." He leaned in and kissed me on my cheek. As he kissed me I felt Queen tighten her arms around my neck. Tiny stars circled around my head and then I saw only black.

I was awakened by a security guard tapping on my window. I don't know how long I had been passed out but my head was throbbing. I wondered for a moment if it had all been a bad dream.

"You can't sleep here." A security guard's pudgy finger tapped at the window. I quickly waved off the guard and started my car. I noticed a letter on my windshield. I hit the button to roll the window down and reached for the note. My heartbeat quickened as I read the note.

Yo ass got a week to get me my money!

Get it or find your home in one of these bayous!

You been warned!

This was like déjà vu.  My past had caught up with the present and the evidence of it was staring me in the face.

***

*With my new found identity I was on the hunt for my new life. I took a long look at my surroundings. Kyra Williams was much too classy to live like this so I made plans to upgrade myself. I decided as soon as Berto dropped off my stuff that I needed to find a safe place for my money. I wasn't gonna be like Redd and have that much cash on me, and I would not be getting my shit from no chop shop.*

*I needed to figure out a way get what I wanted without all the unnecessary questions that went along with dropping that much cash. And if I walked in with that much cash there would be questions. I glanced over at the package I had gotten from Berto, This was the key to my new life. If I wanted to be legit, all of my shit had to appear that way.*

*The next day I decided to test out my fake driver's license at the courthouse to get a DBA. I've done enough research to know what I needed to open a business account. After finishing up with the nice clerk I immediately went to a bank to open an account.*

*I would be able to make larger cash deposits without anyone suspecting anything. Not that the bank should question where the hell I get my money but I thought better of walking into a bank with 500k trying to make a deposit, so over the weeks I funneled money* into my business account. I would make weekly deposits sometimes several times a day for thousands of dollars. I hadn't quite gotten it all in yet but I would.

I had enough to start Kyra on her way. Kyra had her shit together, good education, even better work experience, and exceptional credit. Good, cause you couldn't do a damn thing in today's society without credit. Unless I went back to my old ways and I planned to do a complete 180 with my new found freedom.

Kyra needed a new home, a home to reflect her successful status and a car to go with it. I jumped into my old Nissan. It was time I roll in something a little classier. I remember when Redd gave me the car. I thought I was rolling in style with my leather seats and sunroof, but Redd had me fooled.

The funds he gave me were limited. It was just enough not to fall. I never had anything so everything that he gave me seemed like a lot. While he and his wife were pushing Benz and Bentleys all through the city, I was behind the wheel of a Nissan Altima.

Don't get me wrong, the car was reliable but when it came down to it I deserved the best too. Until I saw how much money he actually kept at my place I had no idea he was bringing in as much as he was. Back home he was at the top of the food chain when it came *to his operation and I knew he was pushing drugs back and forth across state lines, not to mention how he dabbled in providing female companionship for the lonely.*

*I knew if he had that much money stashed at my place there was a lot more where that came from. I knew he kept a stash at his home and his mama house. I didn't know quite how much money he was bringing in but I knew it was a lot. No wonder Queen was ready to kill my ass.*

*I pushed Redd and his money from my thoughts as I arrived at the car dealership. I drove down Interstate 45 until I spotted a place with luxury cars. I looked around assuming I was in north Houston since I was heading north and had been for close to forty-five minutes.*

*The last cross street I saw was FM 1960. I was lost but maybe I was exactly where I needed to be, on one side sat a Mercedes Benz dealership and the other Jaguar.*

*Hmmm. What's a girl to do?*

*I made a quick u-turn and headed towards the Jaguar dealership. A smile crossed my face when I saw all the new toys for me to choose from. Instantly I knew I would be leaving with a new car to match my new attitude.*

# CHAPTER 3

I was walking proof that people are capable of extended periods without sleep. Queen and Redd had caused a rush of adrenaline that kept me in permanent overdrive. This part of my life was supposed to be over with. With each passing year, I gave less thought to the possibility of being found, it had never crossed my mind that my past could catch up with me. I haven't been Dominique Simoneaux in years. I didn't use that name or communicate with anybody from home and no one knew where I was.

My husband knew nothing of my past and that's the way I wanted to keep it. But I wasn't sure how long I could keep my secrets buried if I couldn't get my hands on the money they wanted.

My heart seemed to be constantly in a quickened state. It pounded so hard I was sure I would have a heart attack before this was over. Trent was ignorant to the many misfortunes holding me captive. I wanted so badly to just make them go away, to make them disappear, but I knew without the money they would be a constant part of my life. All those years ago I vowed to change my life and who I am and until now I had done a very good job of being Kyra. I had come too far to turn around. I needed a plan or I was going to lose everything.

I nearly burned a hole into my carpet pacing back and forth. Anxiety flooded my body as I searched for a way out of this abyss but came up with nothing. I couldn't withdraw that much money without it being noticed. I had a little more than 200,000 of the money that I took from Redd. That was my fall back money in case anything ever happened but I kept it in a CD.

I used the money to restart my life. I purchased a car and home and gradually paid them off. I briefly thought of selling the house that we now rent but that would take too long and I would have to answer too many of Trent's questions. If it were one thing Trent was good at was asking questions, it was his job. My only choice would be to break my CD with the bank and pay a hefty penalty. Maybe they would accept a down payment of some sort and allow me to make payments.

The two hundred thousand plus the two hundred fifty-thousand I thought I could slowly take from our joint account would at least be most of the money I had taken. Damn, this was extortion. I thought of going to the police but swiftly dismissed that idea. The thought of me, Kyra Jamison, living under a false identity, and on the run from my former pimp and drug dealer looking to the police for help. I almost wanted to laugh at my damn self. My misdeeds would surely have me sitting behind bars if I tried that.

The sound of the front door opening interrupted my thoughts.

"Hey baby, how was your day?" Maybe asking my husband about his day would take my mind off of the horrible days I've been having.

"Another good day in court! My client was completely exonerated of all charges, didn't even have to do probation." He gloated. He was arrogant, and he loved to win. I imagined those were the things that made him so good in court. He thought that the world was his to own, there was only one way to see it and that was his way.

"Do you think he was guilty?" I was intrigued. I knew what kind of clients he represented. His firm was the one to go to when you need to be acquitted, guilty or not.

"Kyra, why would you ask a thing like that?" A sly smile spread across his lips. "A man is innocent until proven guilty, and prosecution couldn't do that, so my client walks." He still hadn't answered my question. I guessed that was the lawyer in him.

I watched him as he began to remove his clothes. He walked passed me without so much as a kiss. Sometimes I longed for the attention that he used to show me. I know that we have been married for a while but for once I want to feel as special as one of his clients, I wanted the undivided attention he gave his clients, instead of feeling disconnected.

He neatly laid his clothes on the chaise sitting in the corner of our room. My mind wondered as I stared towards that corner. That was the very spot that Redd cornered me in. I could feel the icy touch of his hands on my body. My heart skipped a beat. I had to figure out a way to get rid of them. They were the past and I had no intentions of going backward.

I decided to gather Trent's clothes to take a trip to the cleaners. Every one of my nerve endings was on fire. I couldn't be still and somehow driving always seemed to help me think.

"Our accountant called today." The sound carried through the room, followed by long uncomfortable silence. "There were several purchases made on Saturday and because of the amounts and back to back charges he wanted to make sure that your card hadn't been lost or stolen." He finished. Trent hated when I spent money like that. My back was turned towards him but I could feel his eyes burning into the back of my head.

"Yes, sweetie I went shopping Saturday

remember." I know he didn't remember because I don't believe I told him but that was my defense.

"Well, that must have been some large purchases if he thought the card had been lost or stolen. Just what did you buy?" He stood silently waiting for my answer, but one wasn't coming. Instead, I changed the subject.

"A little of this and that you know, it was a me day. I'm going to run your clothes to the dry cleaners. I'll be back soon." With that said I kissed him on the cheek, grabbed his clothes and moved towards the door.

While driving, the wheels of my mind spun out of control. I attempted to devise a plan to get rid of Redd and his evil wife. My new life had taken me far away from thinking like Dominique. My day today survival used to depend on the hustle, my ability to get over and get out of sticky situations. I needed to find that again, I knew it was somewhere deep inside of me.

My plan of taking the money from our account was out. If the accountant noticed a few purchases he would definitely notice money leaving our account on a regular basis. Driving in circles, I rode the freeways with no destination in mind. Cars sped by me as I traveled along the Sam Houston Tollway. To be honest I wasn't quite sure how I had ended up on the tollway. I exited and turned my car around.

How in the hell had my life turned into this shit show?

I had no desire to return to my old ways. I loved my husband and I believed he loved me. No marriage is perfect but this life is better than the way I was living before. Granted Trent and I had had our problems. There were times I felt devalued and unappreciated.

Even though there was no spontaneous passion constantly erupting between us, I had grown to love him over the years. Most of all he was my safety net. Because of Trent and his profession, I no longer needed or wanted a sugar daddy. I didn't have to prostitute myself for dollars or deal with any of the things I've had to do in my past. Before I was a mistress, now I'm a wife. I supported Trent in his career path, even played a part in catapulting him to success.

I'm married and as the law goes in Texas half of everything he owns was mine. Redd could ruin everything for me and reduce me to nothing. He could expose me, my illegal fake identity, and cause me to lose the only stability I have ever known.

My eyes welled with tears. My emotions seemed to constantly teeter between anger and desperation. I was over this weepy ass bullshit. I realized Kyra needed to take a backseat. It was time to think like Dominique.

"Think girl, think!" I willed myself to become the woman I once was. The by any means necessary chick that showed up and could get out of any fucking situation you pushed her into. It had to be done. Here I was again attempting to get away from Redd and Queen.

I knew I couldn't get them all the money but if I could devise a plan for him to make money I might be able to get rid of him. I snatched my cell phone off of my nightstand and scrolled through my contacts looking for the saved number. I tapped the screen to make the call. I wanted to meet with him.

"You got my money?"

"Maybe I got something better."

"Yeah, well your pussy's good but that shit ain't better than money!" Everything was either sex or money with him.

"I'm not talking about pussy, well I ain't talking about my pussy. Just meet me so we can talk, and leave your wife at home." I hit end after I told him where to meet me.

We decided to meet at a nearby Starbucks. This was the first place I could think of that could manage to be public and private all at the same time. Most of the people were glued to their laptops and tablets. No one would notice us.

I ordered my usual white chocolate mocha and waited. Sitting in the corner I hid behind a magazine while peering over the rim of my shades searching for Redd. I didn't want to be recognized by anyone.

My eyes were glued to Redd as he walked through the door. His toasted sienna colored skin looked as if it had been just kissed by the sun. Redd's dreads were tightly twisted coils that were now much longer than I remembered and his facial hair was neatly lined up. But the thing I found most stunning about this man were his eyes.

The deep green pools could be shockingly hypnotic. Back then he was just my type. He walked with a swagger that said he knew he was the shit and then that's exactly what I wanted. He was a street savvy hustler who turned sex and drugs into a business.

His height commanded the attention of many as he moved through the building. His slender but muscular body wore his clothes well and his row of perfect white teeth peered from under his smile as he noticed me in the corner. Those piercing eyes watched me as he sank into his seat.

"So do you have my money?" The words rolled from his lips, jolting me back into the present. He wasted no time getting to business.

"I have some of your money."

"Some is not all baby, don't you think your time will be better spent by getting me the rest of my money!" Redd's smile was almost a snarl.

"I already told you I can't move that type of money from our account. It would be noticed." Trent's observation was a gentle reminder me that he's always watching the finances. It would be a stupid move on my part to go anywhere near that account to repay my debt.

"So what you want, to try in talk me out of getting my money, well forget it. You stole from me and I want what's mine. I need it." The tone of his voice told me he did need it. He was desperate for it, and desperate men did desperate things.

"Look Redd, I didn't have a choice, your wife threatened to kill me." I felt a need to explain. I never had a chance to give my version of events. I'm sure Queen's story was unfairly skewed in her favor.

"You had a choice, you made it and never looked back. Now you have another choice to make. Either get me my money or deal with the consequences. I think you have a lot more to lose than I do when hubby finds you're not exactly who you claim to be. Once he knows who you really are and leaves your ass, I'll come again to collect, but the next time payment will be your life."

I decided I'd had enough of this conversation and tried to steer it in another direction. I needed to run my plan by him and get him to agree. This was a way to get us what we both wanted. I wanted silence and he wanted money, I knew my plan could bring him that and then some.

"Hey, you remember back in the day when sex was your big business?" I didn't want to say pimp even though I guess that's what it was. He wasn't what you thought of when you thought of a pimp, he wasn't smackin' hoes or taking all of their money, he was good at providing horny men with sexual pleasure and I had a plan to take his know how and my expertise to build a business that would make money fast and quickly remove him from my life.

"What does that have to do with anything?" I could hear the annoyance in his voice. Once he got in the drug game he pretty much abandoned prostitution.

"It has to do with everything." I smiled. "Let me build you the best little whorehouse in Texas."

***

I cruised the streets in my brand new Jaguar feeling like a new woman, a reinvented woman. I shed my old skin and the new person I was wasn't going to be a gutter girl any longer. These degrees Berto got me were the real deal, stamped signed and sealed by the school. I don't know who his connect was, but they were damn good.

It wasn't hard to get an interview with Wells Fargo, I was hired on the spot after feeding them everything that was typed on the resume that was prepared for me. With all my credentials, they would have been foolish not to hire me.

After my interview, I found a gorgeous apartment and put a deposit. I was informed that a decision would be made after a credit check. I smiled when they said that knowing there would be no problem with Kyra Williams credit. Within hours my phone was ringing telling me I had the apartment. Things were finally looking up for me. I loved being Kyra.

I admit I was a bit concerned about Redd, if he found me I'm sure he would kill me. So I devised a plan that would keep him busy for a while. I reached for my new cell phone and made a call. My fingers trembled as I touched the keypad. I dialed the number on a card I received when Redd was being investigated.

*It had been at the bottom of my purse for ages. I didn't know then it would come in handy and I actually never planned on using it. Whenever they tried to approach me about Redd I denied even knowing him. When it came to Redd I was loyal. I would have never turned on him, but now I saw things differently.*

*"May I speak with Detective Bradford?"*

*"Speaking." The voice that hissed back was less than patient.*

*"Hello, I received your card a few months ago concerning Lawrence Richardson, I have some information that may be of value to you." His long pause told me I had gotten his attention. I even think he put down his doughnut for a moment.*

*"Who is this?"*

*"Just know that I'm someone who can help you." I didn't care to leave my name. I went on to tell him information that only I was privy to. Not enough to get Redd locked up, just enough to give the police a reason to look and him a reason to hide. If the plan went my way, Redd would so busy with keeping them law off his back he wouldn't worry about me. In time, I hoped he would forget all about me and the money I took.*

# CHAPTER 4

Redd readily agreed with my plan of creating Houston's very on Bunny Ranch. Any plan that made him money made him smile. My little plan was now in motion. I cashed in my CD and agreed to meet with Redd today to find a suitable space for our joint venture.

I maneuvered my car into a nearby parking spot across from the apartments Redd and Queen shared. My eyes roamed the area taking in all that I saw. This area reminded me of one the first areas I lived in. The rent was cheap and the area was rough.

Redd moved slowly across the street as if he wore a bumper. Blowing horns and shouting drivers cursed Redd as he made his way to the car. Once he spotted my car he opened the door and got in.

"What's up D?" His lips curled into a seductive smile and I instantly knew what that look meant.

I rolled my eyes ignoring his adolescent attempts to lure me into his arms. We wouldn't be talking about anything unless it was about business. I knew better than to open that door. There was too much history between us.

Whenever I got around Redd I became incredibly nervous. There was no doubt in my mind that I loved Trent. Being with him had changed my entire world, but when Redd was near my body involuntarily reacted.

Heat rushed to my face as I inhaled his sultry scented cologne. I didn't want him to know he had that affect on me. I was doing my damnedest to hide it. Curiosity got the better of me as I shifted my eyes to look at Redd. The straight leg jeans he wore were dark in some areas and faded in others and his shoes were as white as the winter snow.

The aviator style Gucci sunglasses reflected my profile. He was watching me watch him. I quickly turned my attention to the traffic in front of me, pissed that he caught me watching him. Damn he looked good.

I zipped my car in and out of traffic trying to get to our destination and get out of this car. I needed him out of my personal space. His presence was suffocating me, surrounding me so much I could not catch my breath. I exhaled, trying to slow my quickened pulse when I felt the tender touch of his slender fingers inch up the length of my leg. He acted as if I wouldn't notice. He cautiously rubbed my thigh, almost as if asking permission by the hesitation in his touch. My thighs tightened as I felt the stir of arousal between my legs. His touch, although I hadn't felt it in years, was familiar against my skin.

Everything inside of me signaled that this was a bad idea. I needed to get rid of him and allowing this would make that even harder. The voice in my head screamed again and again to stop this, but the words never escaped my lips.

My body craved the rush that he was giving me. I struggled to keep control of the car as Redd pushed my legs apart and worked his way to my inner thigh. His powerful hand moved seductively until he found my lace panties. I wanted to succumb to the desire, to allow this man to touch me in every way I remembered but that inner voice finally snapped me back to reality.

"Stop!"

"Don't act like you don't like it." He smiled slyly as the words to tumble from his lips.

"It's not about whether I want it or not. It's about what's right and wrong and this ain't right. I'm married and just in case you forgot so are you." My eyes darted at him as I drove, angry at him for trying to cross that line, and even angrier with myself for wanting him to.

"That never stop you before." He sounded offended.

"Maybe I'm not the same person as before." We drove the rest of the way to meet the realtor in silence. Thankfully, he kept his hands to himself. I stilled tingled between my legs from our close encounter.

Nestled in a wooded area was a gorgeous two-story home. There was a large iron gate that stood open and allowed entrance into the driveway. As I drove the semi-circular path I noticed the manicured lawn. The curved driveway led me to the front of the house where I stopped the car and parked behind the realtor's car.

I knew before even seeing the inside this was perfect. Secluded from all, this would be the perfect place to run his business. Part of me couldn't believe that I was helping him, but the survivor in me would do anything to ensure my well being.

I stepped out the car and walked towards the front door. The sprawling double doors were edged in cherry colored wood with the center being a mixture of bronze and glass uniting to create a breathtaking design. The shady realtor's chatter was merely background noise as I stepped into the house. I pretended to listen as he went through his sales pitch.

I really didn't understand why he was going through the motions of actually trying to sell us the house, he should have known through our connect, that this deal was as good as closed. This realtor's only real job was ensuring our names weren't connected to anything. If things ever got out of control the paper trail would lead to some nameless person that probably didn't exist.

Stepping back into my old world was both familiar and foreign. I watched as Redd and the realtor eagerly probed every inch of this house. I broke away from the group and began to roam the halls alone. I needed time to focus on how the hell I would pull this off. I stumbled across a long hallway which led me to the master bedroom. It's impressive size overwhelmed me and instantly the wheels of my mind started to turn.

We could use this room as the presidential suite or VIP room, and we could charge a ton for it. My heels sank into the plush carpet as I made my way to the bathroom. In the center sat a sunken marble jacuzzi bathtub. The left side of the room was completely mirrored from floor to ceiling and the marble countertops matched the tub and shower tiles perfectly. I stood in silence and contemplated the possibilities. I was so lost in my own thoughts I didn't hear when Redd walked in behind me.

I could see his reflection in the mirror, watching me watch him. He closed the space between us, never saying a word, then I felt the strength of his embrace around my waist. It was always Redd's unexpected desire for me that drove me wild. It was something I craved, but

Trent was rarely spontaneous.

"Can you still do that thing with your tongue?" Redd whispered into my ear. Memories of our past caused a slow smile to spread across my face. It felt good to be wrapped in his arms. Just like before, my mind told me to stop him, but part of me that refused. Somewhere I still loved this man. At one time I craved him, needed him, and wanted to be his everything. My eyes closed as my body gave in to the kisses he planted along my neck.

Without thinking, I turned towards him and found his supple lips. Our tongues teasingly united as we kissed. His right hand moved up my spine ending at the nape of my neck before provocatively pulling my head back. He lifted me onto the marble counter and pulled my skirt around my waist. His fingers eagerly probed the fleshy folds between my legs. Years have passed since I felt this man touch me but it was as if he remembered every spot that triggered a response.

"So if you're not the same old Dominique, why are you so wet?" His piercing eyes probed me, waiting for an answer. He waited, but there was no response. I didn't have an answer. I wasn't the same person, at least I hadn't been in all these years but now Dominique was surfacing and I couldn't stop her.

My left leg dangled to the floor while Redd

held the other. He dropped down to one knee and pushed his face towards my center. He slid my lace undies to the side while his tongue swirled and pushed from left to right. I shivered with delight as he brought me to the brink of orgasm and then pulled away, which only intensified my desire for him.

Our eyes connected as I ran my tongue across his lips, savoring my own juices. I heard the rip of tearing fabric, but I couldn't care less about the expensive lingerie. I watched as the wispy fabric floated to the floor. I blindly reached for his pants and undid his button and zipper. I reached inside and wrapped my hand around the warm thickness that swelled even more as I touched him. My hands ran the length of his shaft repeatedly before tenderly rubbing the tip of my thumb across the head.

"Damn." He groaned signaling he was ready to feel more than just my hands on him. I pulled his pants further down completely exposing him. He rubbed against my clit, teasing me, denying us both the pleasure we obviously desperately craved.

"You ready for me."

"Yes."

Inch by inch I could feel him fill me completely. My body felt the sting of both pleasure and pain as my body opened up to receive him. Somewhere in the back of my mind, someone was screaming stop, but it was a faint whisper compared to the voice that called for this man's touch.

"I know you missed this good dick!" Redd breathed into my ear. "Say it, tell me you missed Daddy's dick!" He demanded, but I wouldn't speak. I didn't want to give him the satisfaction of knowing no one could touch me the way he could. Redd was always so spontaneous, so fulfilling. He moved faster, thrusting harder with each stroke.

He slowed his pace and pushed deep inside of me. My hands tightened across his back before moving upward to pull his lips towards mine. Our tongues danced as our passion took control of us. With this man, every way he stroked me was the right way. My body allowed all of him, swallowing every inch as he moved in and out of me.

"Say it, I know you love me, and you love the way I fuck you!" He still demanded more of me. I began to move my hips in sync with his thrust. I pushed, he pushed, and my breast bounced to the beat of our lovemaking.

"Damn, you feel good!" Redd whispered into my ear before running his tongue across my lips. I could tell he was about to climax, his strokes became more intense. He even felt harder as he tapped the bottom. I wrapped my legs around his waist, pulling him even closer.

His hand clasped around my neck. My body stilled in obedience with his unspoken command. Short gasps slipped from my lips as I became overwhelmed with pleasure. My skin developed tiny bumps as we became more intense. He took my erect nipples into his mouth, lightly biting them. My entire body tensed and shuddered. I could feel the warm juices flowing from my middle, down my thighs and onto him as I came. I finally opened my eyes as Redd began to cum, he pulled me even closer as he released himself inside of me.

My weakened body tumbled against Redd. I needed to catch my breath. I blinked twice trying to focus. Redd had my mind so gone I completely forgot about the realtor, but he hadn't forgotten about us. In the shadows of the doorway he stood, watching us as he held himself in silence.

***

*Making that call to the police was one of the best ideas I had. That would get Redd off of my back, he would be too busy with the police to worry about me or his money.*

*Today was my first week at my new job. I was bored out of my mind and quickly attempted to learn what my resume said I already knew. I did learn one part of my job quickly and that was delegating. All that I couldn't figure out I designated another employee in my department to complete. Sitting at my desk I reviewed tons and tons of accounts.*

*I needed to get out of this place. I hadn't had a real job in so long that sitting at this desk was driving me crazy. I grabbed my purse and walked towards the door, just as I was going out a man was coming in. The door swung open so wide I was knocked off balance and fell to the ground. My first response was to jump up and whip his ass. I know that's what Dominique would do, but I had to think about what Kyra would do.*

*"I'm so sorry." His deep voice captivated me. He extended his hand towards me as a gesture to help me to my feet. His smile was alluring. He gazed at me with chestnut brown eyes, coffee colored skin and an immaculate body that showed through his expertly tailored suit.*

"What's the hurry?" I said as I attempted to dust myself off and straighten my clothes. I guess he found my comment funny because he chuckled. He still had not released my hand.

"I apologize, really, let me make it up to you by treating you to lunch." He offered. I didn't know this man from Adam, but that didn't mean I didn't want to get to know him and a girl's gotta eat. I tilted my head to the side watching him out of the corner of my eye.

"Can you start by telling me your name and then maybe I will consider lunch." I stared in silence, not wanting my eyes to give away how I truly felt about lunch with him.

"I'm Trent Jamison." He handed me a business card as he spoke. I agreed to lunch and found myself walking with him and completely swept away by his conversation. We talked, and not the kind of talking that Redd and I did. Not street talk, so to speak, it was real talk.

He told me how he was fresh out of law school and working for one of the biggest law firms as a junior associate. He continued to talk, possibly in an attempt to impress me. What he didn't realize is the more he talked about him. The less I would have to talk about me.

# CHAPTER 5

After I dropped Redd off at his apartment I used my alone time to think. I was embarrassed by my actions and I couldn't understand what had come over me. Perhaps the excitement and nostalgia of it all had caused me to lose every last one of my senses.

With Redd's return into my life, I had to think and act like I did when the streets were my home, but that definitely didn't mean I wanted to rekindle that type of relationship with him. I was done with being Redd's faithful concubine, years away had shown me I was capable of better.

I pulled my car into the garage and breathed a sigh of relief when I saw I was home alone. Piece by piece I began to pull my clothes from my body as I headed towards the shower. Somehow I thought I could wash away my illicit behavior. No matter how much I desired Redd, no matter how much chemistry we had, I could never allow what happened between us to happen again.

I found comfort in my bed. I enveloped myself in my blankets welcoming the quiet comfort. I gazed at the ceiling intently, hoping that somehow the answers to my problems were there.    I tapped the home button of my iPhone to check the time. It was after midnight, where was Trent?

Maybe he is just working late.

It wasn't enough room in my brain at the moment to worry where Trent was. Thoughts ran a marathon in my mind as I assessed the day's events.  I couldn't believe I had allowed myself to get caught up with Redd. The very thought of going to back to those days repulsed me and I could not understand why I had succumbed to my desires. When I left Louisiana I still loved Redd.

I thought the years and distance would put an end to my fairytale ideas of our love, and until now I thought it had. One thing was accomplished though. We had found a place for his business. I knew I didn't need Redd as apart of my life anymore, but for some reason, I felt confused.When you know better you're supposed to do better, but every time I thought of the way he touched me my body trembled. Being around him allowed all of my old feelings to surface, which I truly didn't want and thinking of what happened today only made it worst.

I found myself so aroused I had to touch myself. I allowed my hands to fall below the covers. Slowly I made my way to my center, thinking of the feeling of ecstasy I was lost in today.

I touched myself, feeling all of my moistness. My nipples swelled with the anticipation of my own touch as I moved my hands slowly, teasing myself.

The sound of the bedroom door opening interrupted me. Trent's movements were catlike as he moved through the room. His steps were extra cautious in an attempt not to wake me. I could either pretend to be sleep or get satisfaction for this burning between my legs. I decided to get satisfaction. Maybe if I directed my energy and desire towards my husband, it wouldn't leave room for my lust for Redd.

I moved the comforter away from my body. "Trent?" I called to him, hoping he would move towards the sound of my voice.

"Hey, I didn't know you were awake." He almost sounded disappointed.

"I'm awake. Why don't you come put me to sleep?" I said in the most seductive voice I could find. I remember there was a time this man was insanely excited at the thought of touching my body. Now at times it seemed as if it were a bit of a nuisance.

"Can you wait until I get out of the shower?" He said.

"I would prefer if you would come extinguish this fire now!" I slowly removed my gown and stood in front of him. Our room was chilly and my nipples stood at attention. I moved closer to him to rub against him. The closer I moved to him, the further he stepped away.

I touched his smooth skin and pulled his hand towards the bed. "Make love to me." He pulled back and stood away from the bed.

"I will make love to you, but first I'm taking a shower." He swiftly moved towards the bathroom, closed the door and locked it. I stood in the middle of the floor, naked and baffled. There was a knot forming in the pit of my stomach. I felt rejected and I didn't understand why it was imperative that he take a shower at this very moment. It's not like he works outside, he sits at a desk and in courtrooms.

Feeling defeated, I climbed in my bed, beckoning the comfort of sleep to take away the sting of my rejection. After what seemed like hours I heard the bathroom door open. The freshness of his newly cleansed body invaded the room. I felt Trent climb into the bed. His hands gently rubbed my thighs as he tried to pull me close to him.

My eyes were closed so I didn't have to make eye contact with him, and I didn't respond to his probing hands. Pretending to be sleep, I never so much as peaked at him. Eventually, he got the message and decided to go to sleep. At least one of us could sleep because I couldn't. Trent didn't usually make me feel rejected, perhaps ignored at times but I know that's because he is consumed with work.

This felt different. I had never had a reason to question Trent's feelings for me, but tonight left me in a totally different place. I turned my back to Trent and looked at the clock. It was three in the morning and I knew I had a long day ahead of me. I closed my eyes tight, praying for sleep.

The next morning I awoke in an empty bed. Saturday mornings Trent usually slept in but he was long gone. I pushed my hand towards the nightstand and shuffled its contents from left to right until I found my phone and dialed Trent. It rang once and quickly went to voicemail. That was odd but I didn't have time to figure it out.

Perhaps he went to the gym. I jumped up and prepared myself for the day. The fact that he wasn't here was a plus. That meant that he couldn't question me. I stumbled to our walk-in closet and found attire for the day. Still struggling against sleep I groggily stumbled into the bathroom and tapped the faucet to turn on the water. I doused my face with the warm refreshing liquid.

I grabbed my runaway locks and pulled them into a ponytail as I applied make up. I wanted to feel sexy today. No, I needed to feel sexy today. Redd insisted I shop with him for home decor. I should have said no but he had me in a bit of a bind. I couldn't believe I had handed that man two hundred thousand dollars without so much as blinking my eye.

Well, yes the hell I could, I think if I wouldn't have I might have really been found in a bayou somewhere. I was trying to buy my way to freedom. Once he started making money he was going to let me go. He better let me go.

On my way to meet Redd I decided I needed to talk to him about my debt. We needed a mutual understanding. I parked in the same spot I had when we had gone to view the house. I noticed him standing near his apartment, talking with a man. I don't know what they were talking about but whatever it was it looked serious. He moved in almost a jog to the car.

"What it do D?" He said as he opened the door and climbed into the car.

"Hey Redd, what's up?" I was dry as hell. I didn't want him to think we were about to start round two.

"You!"

"No, I'm not, look I think that we need to talk. What happened yesterday can't happen again. Ever. I don't want to go down that road again and have your crazy ass wife looking to kill my ass." I could tell by the expression on his face he wasn't trying to hear what I was saying. Silence fell over the car as he glared at me. I drove in silence for a moment before I spoke again. "You have to agree that this is about business."

"I don't have to agree with shit. I don't know what makes you think you calling the shots, I'm in control of this here, just like I've always been!"

"You need to lower your voice, like I said, I'm just trying to make sure that the things that happened yesterday don't ever happen again. This is business and when you start making your money back, I'm out. Hell, I've given you half the money I owe you. Paid your down payment for your house and handed you the rest of your money. How well you do is up to you."

"You got that wrong baby girl, it's up to you too. If I don't make my money then you'll be working for me forever. I don't know why you don't just relax and enjoy the ride. This was your idea, remember. " He smiled and moved his hands towards my legs. He gently squeezed my thigh as he gazed at me.

"Stop it damn it, I told you that shit was over, this is strictly business." I pushed his hands away from me. Even though I moved fast, he moved faster. Redd grabbed the steering wheel.

"Stop it!"

"Pull this shit over right now!" He was so forceful it scared me. I didn't plan on being in an accident today so I turned down a dead end and pulled over. Even though it was daylight, being in a wooded dead end scared the hell out of me.

"What is wrong with you? Don't do that, you could have killed us both." I inhaled deeply, I was finding it hard to catch my breath.

"Get out the fuckin' car!" His gaze was so intense it paralyzed me. I guess I didn't move fast enough because before I knew it my car door was flying open and I was being yanked out of the car by my hair. My legs struggled to keep up with the fast pace of his tugging. I fell to my knees unable to firmly plant my feet on the ground.

Redd peered down at me before grabbing me and pulling me to my feet as if I were his puppet. I faced him defiantly. I wasn't going to give him the satisfaction of letting him know I was scared as hell. That's what this asshole wanted. He shoved me towards the car and pushed my face against the hood. The heat from the car stung as my bare skin pressed against the metal. I felt probing hands under my skirt as he found my panties and yanked them away from my body.

"Redd, stop." I attempted to stand but he shoved me back down while pushing my skirt around my waist. I struggled to push him off me, but Redd grabbed my hands and restrained them behind my back. I was now his prisoner.

"Pleas stop, don't do this." I pleaded with him to stop. I couldn't see his face, but his forceful motions told me he wasn't listening.

"I'm not stopping, you want me just as much as I want you. We're not over Dominique, not until I say we are." He pushed himself inside of me. I could hear cars speeding by as he moved in and out of me. I knew I should have stopped him. I shouldn't have allowed myself to be bent over the hood of a car in the middle of the day, having sex with someone who was not even my husband.

I wanted to scream rape, but that's only what my mind said. My body was calling for every thrust he gave me. His hands held me tight, inflicting just enough pain to arouse me even more.

"Yeah, you like that dick, say it!" Yesterday I hadn't given him the satisfaction of verbalizing what my body knew. Today was different though. His forceful, take it nature drove me over the edge. As he pushed in and out of me the wetter I felt myself getting. Before long I was meeting his thrust, rolling my hips in eager delight.

He released my hands and allowed me to grip the hood as he dove deeper and deeper in me. The thought of being caught or watched by people driving by only made me want this man more.

Redd pulled himself away from me and turned me around. My bare ass now sat on the warm hood as he found his way inside. I still hadn't allowed myself to speak but I didn't know how much I could take before my mouth gave away what my body was feeling.

"Say it. You love this dick don't you!" His commands were persistent.

"I love that dick!" Moans escaped my lips as I came. My body was motionless as I lie on the hood of my car, a car that my husband gave me and paid for. The funny thing was, even though I knew I should have felt bad for what I just did, sexual ecstasy would not allow me.

***

*Meeting Trent had completely changed my outlook on what I wanted in a man. He was different from all of the guys that I met before and that's probably what I liked about him. When I was Dominique, I looked for the guys with the fattest pockets, the biggest dick, and the street rep to match.*

*But now, I wanted to do things a little different. I mean look at where my choice in man had gotten me. I was away from everyone and everything I loved. At times I longed for home, but between Redd and Queen looking for me, I knew I wouldn't be going anytime soon.*

*I sat at Starbucks waiting for Trent to show up for our afternoon coffee break. We worked so close to one another that this had become a daily thing for us. I got to know him and I can say I liked what I saw. So what he didn't walk with street swag and his attire was clean and tailored instead of jeans and kicks. I did like the way he made me feel.*

*While waiting my cell phone rang and broke my peaceful silence. I looked at the caller id and noticed the 504 area code. Shit. Why would anyone be calling me from 504? I trusted no one enough to give them my number, not even my mother. As far as the state of Louisiana was concerned, Dominique Simoneaux had disappeared never to be heard of again.*

Curiosity won  and I answered the phone.

"Hello."

"Who is this?"  A husky voice spoke to me. "You know it doesn't even matter, I have a message for you. Mind your fuckin' business! Shit don't stay anonymous in Detective Bradford's precinct. I got your number, and soon Redd will know who you are and where you are so if I were you I would sleep with one eye open bitch!"

The phone line went dead.  My hands trembled as I placed the phone down.  Trent had walked up during this conversation.

"What's wrong baby?"  I couldn't even answer. I didn't know how they had gotten my number but somebody had it.  I knew I would cancel this cell phone before I had made it back to my desk.

Trent stood over me still concerned.  I couldn't let that call get to me.  Houston was a big place, and obviously they didn't know who I was they only had the number. I be damn if I run again. If Redd came after me, he would damn sure get a run for his money. If he found me it would be because I slipped, and I didn't plan on slipping.

# CHAPTER 6

Two weeks have passed since my encounter with Redd. I was preparing to see him tonight, which was supposed to be about business but with Redd it always ended up personal. I had not been intimate with my husband since our spontaneous shower session, and that bothered me a little, but Redd made sure to keep me busy so I couldn't worry too much about Trent.

I sat at my vanity table and watched Trent gather his things for a shower. He walked in and immediately moved towards the bathroom. Usually, he would undress in the bedroom and neatly arrange his clothes over the chair for me to gather and take to the cleaners. That didn't happen tonight. Odd, extremely odd. I leaned against the bathroom door and scanned the room for his clothes.

"Hey baby, where are your clothes? I'm getting them ready for the cleaners." I saw where his clothes were sitting but I was more interested in his response than his clothes.

"You know baby, don't worry about it, I will take the clothes to the cleaners." I watched him through the glass as he took his shower. There has been something very strange about his behavior. He never took clothes to the cleaners. Honestly, Trent never did any of the things he deemed trivial. He left that to his dutiful wife to do.

"So you got room for me in that shower?"

"Actually baby I'm about to get out." He stepped out and swiftly kissed me on my cheek then pushed passed me. I stood in the doorway by myself. I didn't really want to take a shower, I just wanted my husband to respond to me in a way that said he wanted me. But nowadays, it just felt as if he were trying to push me away.

He has left me with the feeling of rejection one too many times. He honestly didn't realize who the hell he was messing with. I walked back to my vanity and continued to apply my make-up. I was leaving, if Trent needed space, it would be space he got. Redd and I were doing a bit of business scouting. I started gathering my clothes but it was as if Trent didn't even notice that I was leaving; did he even care?

I finished my makeup and headed to put my clothes on and grabbed a pair of heels. I stepped in front of my full length mirror to inspect my appearance. The woman that stared back at me oozed confidence and sex appeal. The black faux leather skirt I wore was fitting, and hugging every curve of my body. My dark sheer shirt hung loosely at my waist. The deep v-neck exposed my silver bra.

"I'm leaving," I said as I closed the garage door. I didn't give Trent time to answer me let alone question me about where I'm going. In the exact same spot I always waited in, I watched as Redd left his apartment. Queen stood at the door, planting a kiss on his lips before he exited.

The sight of those two in a tender embrace made me nauseous. Kyra shouldn't care one way or another but Dominique didn't like to see them all over each other. Whatever. I discarded the thoughts of them from my mind. I had my own man to worry about.

"Let me drive tonight," Redd said through the open door.

"I can't let you drive my car."

"Yes, you can, get out and let me drive you tonight." I thought about all the things that could go wrong by letting him drive my car. Forget it. I stepped out of the car and climbed into the passenger side. I was tired of playing chauffeur. I let my seat back and enjoyed the ride. Redd looked towards me and as always he touched my thighs.

"So you gone give Daddy a taste of that tonight?" Redd asked.

"You sure you only need a taste?" I flirtatiously laughed as I shifted in the seat, exposing my legs just a bit more. I planned to have a good time tonight. No worries about home or how strange Trent was acting. I reclined in the seat and sank into the smooth plush leather. Slowly my old personality was gradually becoming dominant.

Tonight was supposed to be about business, but I just wanted to have a good time. Redd parked the car and before I could open my door he was at the door helping me out. We walked in side by side. The smoked filled room was warm as nearly nude females walked the floor.

It was Redd's idea to find our talent in a strip club. I guess some girls would be willing to do anything for a quick buck, I used to be one of them and in some way I still am. Coming to a strip club is not something my husband would ever think of doing, and definitely not with me. Redd led me to a VIP room in the back of the club.

I felt all eyes on me as I moved seductively beside Redd. We were a couple to be admired. I tossed my hair as my hips rocked to the beat of the music. Once we reached the room I sat down, crossed my legs and requested a drink. I needed a little something to take the edge off.

Sipping on my drink, I watched as one of the girls entered the room. She bared a striking resemblance to Beyonce. Layered golden tresses fell to her shoulders as she undid her hair clip. Her eyes shifted my way and then to Redd before fully entering the room. She knew she was here for an interview. Redd knew the owner of the club and he had given us a list of girls willing to work, keep their legs open and their mouths closed.

She stood in the middle of the floor watching me. I could feel her eyes roam my body practically pleading with me to look directly at her. Her body glistened with hues of gold. Sipping on my drink I never gave her the eye contact she desired. She moved slowly, seductively; exuding sexiness with each step.

"I'm Obsession." Her voice was sweet yet sultry. She moved towards Redd. The point of these meetings was to get a feel for the girls. To see what they looked like and how they moved. Obviously, Obsession had a plan of her own. With each step she took she removed a piece of clothing. Not that she was wearing all that much. By the time she reached Redd she was completely naked.

This woman's body was the epitome of beauty, it was the kind of body that women envied in the gym. She was a bronze colored goddess that moved as if she was floating across the room. Her brown skin was smooth and rich. She kneeled before Redd and with one quick movement was swallowing him whole.

I didn't even see her pull it out. I watched her technique. She watched me. I would be lying if I said this didn't turn me on. Redd rested comfortably against his chair with his head back. I could tell he was enjoying this.

I squirmed in my seat, my legs crossing and uncrossing my legs. My nipples hardened and pulse quickened.The more I watched, the hotter I became. My hands traced lines along my thighs. She saw me watching her and began to really put on a show. She pulled a Magnum from I don't know where and ripped the package open.

She straddled Redd backward, placed the condom on the tip, unrolling it with her hand as she lowered herself on to him. This chick had tricks and shit. She bounced up and down and her hips rocked back and forth. Redd threw his head back and gripped her hips. He pulled her into him forcefully and if the look on her face was any indication, she was enjoying every bit of it. The more she took it the harder he gave it. I watched as he eyes rolled, his body shook and he grabbed her hips in an attempt to hold on for a wild ride.

Just before he reached his climax, she stood. I could see him glistening with her juices. She stepped back and slowly walked towards me. My pulse quickened with anxiety and anticipation as she closed the space between us. Her moving my way scared the shit out of me. She didn't wait for permission to touch me, she simply took it.

She leaned towards me, touching my chin to slowly lift me towards her, then kissed me. Her kiss was tender and sweet, but full of passion and desire. Her tongue moved with mine. It was so intense it made me weak. She was working her way down my neck and to my breast.

Being with another woman was something completely new to me. She spread my legs as Redd positioned himself behind her. Obsession was now on her knees with her head nestled between my legs. I could feel the swiftness of her tongue as it traced tiny circles along my clit.

Redd locked eyes with me as he slid inside of her. Her body jerked as he pushed further inside of her. She worked her tongue and he worked her. Her fingers now moved in and out of me, causing my muscles to tighten. I could feel myself about to climax. She pushed her hips back to meet each of his strokes. The harder he pushed from the back, the further her fingers thrust inside of me.

I couldn't take it anymore, the stimulation was too strong and I succumbed to this wonderful feeling. Redd wasn't far behind, I could tell he was about to cum. He swiftly slid himself out of Obsession and released a steady stream of his seed onto her apple shaped ass.

Obsession was a woman who truly knew

her profession. She was definitely hired. After she left we saw a few girls but none as impressive as Obsession. We made a list of the ones we wanted to work with and they would meet us tomorrow at the house. Everything seemed to fall into place.

***

I have to admit, when I received the call from back home it scared the crap out of me. I retired that part of my life, but here it was again staring me in my face. Needless to say, I threw that phone in the trash, and immediately went to Trent and persuaded him to add me to his account as a share plan.

Knowing the kind of dude he is, the old me would have taken advantage of him. I would have taken him for everything and left him broke, busted and confused, but Kyra did things a little different. I would allow him to stick around. I wanted him to stay.

I had plans on us being together but before we could I needed his pockets to be a little fatter. As a junior associate he didn't make shit and I didn't have time to be the doting wife in the corner watching him climb the corporate ladder. I couldn't deal with that.

I wanted to do things differently but one thing I couldn't deal with was a broke ass struggling man. I saw potential in us as a couple, with me pushing him we could be a power couple, the couple that all envied.

Today I was meeting Trent for lunch in his office. When I walked in I noticed a salt and peppered haired man eyeing me. Mmm, I see he likes a little chocolate swirl in his vanilla. I smiled. Trent was walking towards me. As we left to the break room I heard him speak to old, gray haired guy. I soon figured out this dude was in charge . He watched me as he stopped and chatted with Trent. They talked about boring stuff that held no interest to me.

I could feel old guys eyes, roam over my body. While I watched him watching me the wheels in my head began to turn. I know I told myself I was going to become a new person, but perhaps I could employ some of my old techniques to help my new man get ahead. He just needed a chance.

As we moved towards the break room, I looked over my shoulder and winked at the salt and peppered haired man. When I did that he smiled and turned beet red. I licked my lips and blew kisses at him while Trent talked about getting some type of promotion. If I had my way he would get more than a promotion. I am talking corner office and partner status.

"Trent baby, who is he?" I tilted my head towards the man.

"Oh, that's our founding partner, Jacob. Smith. Let me introduce you two."

Trent introduced us, completely oblivious to mister salt and pepper's hidden desire. It didn't matter. I just needed a way in. A signal to him that he could have what he wanted, for *the right price.*

*Our introduction was short. Trent and I turned to leave but Mr. Smith never took his eyes off of me. He continued to watch me, so I put an extra little twist in my hips. He was losing his damn mind. I knew it was a matter of time before I could get him to do anything I wanted him to do.*

# CHAPTER 7

I was headed down a dangerous path. Redd did something to me, he did something for me. It was like old times. There was a time when I felt like he was my best friend. He was my man and my everything. It didn't matter to me that he was married. I never saw it that way. I knew he was with her, I even played my position but in my mind, he always belonged to me.

I sat on the edge of my bed consumed by my thoughts and overwhelmed with confusion. Lawrence Richardson was nothing but trouble. He was as unstable as a schizophrenic on crack. Like a ticking bomb he could explode at any moment. I had to keep myself from going there.

I watched Trent as he slept. We hadn't been together sexually in weeks. I hadn't even noticed because I was being fulfilled by Redd. I knew this was ridiculous and I didn't want to be caught in the situation. Trapped between two men, wanting to be with them both.

Dismissing those thoughts from my head I moved towards our closet. There was no need to burden myself with thoughts of things I couldn't change. My past was kicking my ass. I had to get Redd off of it and keep Trent from knowing.

I was more than accustomed to my lifestyle and if Trent ever found out who I really was I would lose everything.

I dressed for our meeting with the girls. There would be six girls to start. That was more than enough. Everyone was supposed to be in attendance, even Queen. I didn't want her anywhere around me but Redd insisted. She knew people from working at the law firm, and she was given the task of spreading the word to those she knew would be more than willing to pay for it.

The plan was to target lawyers and judges, athletes and business owners. People who could lose everything just for knowing about this place. I slipped out the house unnoticed. On my way there I made a mental note to surprise Trent for lunch at his office. There was a time we had lunch together every day, but it has been so long since we have been able to. I guess we have been so consumed with ourselves we haven't taken the time to think about each other.

Getting caught up in this crazy life didn't make matters any better, but I felt that I had to fight for my new life. I was playing the survival game and I wasn't prepared to lose.

I parked my car and briefly admired the home. The home that my money had purchased. I remember eagerly handing over money to Redd, eager to get him out of my life, but now

I'mm conflicted.

"Got damn it!" I know this bitch didn't just slap me. I didn't know what the hell her problem was but we weren't about to start this again. My first response was to grab my face but as soon as I realized she slapped me I lunged for her throat.

"What the hell is your problem?" My hands desperately sought to strangle her. Redd jumped between us as many of the girls watched in amusement. My arms stretched around him desperately trying to strangle her

"You are my problem, bitch you have always been my problem!" I had no idea what was going on. I walked through the door and was greeted with a hand. "And you Redd, why you takin' up for the bitch, move out my damn way."

He stood as a wall between her and I. This was the very last time she was going to put her hands on me and get away with it. When she saw that Redd wasn't budging she went around him and walked towards the door.

As soon as she walked by I stuck my foot out causing her to trip and fall into the wall. She wasn't going to keep putting her hands on me and threatening me. I was ready for a fight. At one point Queen did somewhat intimidate me, but things were different now. She was no longer going to intimidate me with her Queen Bee status. She wasn't Queen of the hood anymore. She didn't have dumb young girls eager to prove they were loyal to her anymore.

Redd helped Queen to her feet and pushed her towards the door. She watched me as she walked away. Her eyes were daggers that cut me with every piercing glance. I was frozen ready for a fight if she tried to bring it. As far as things between Queen and I, shit would be changing. I was damn sure tired of her putting her hands on me when she felt like it, and then Redd always jumping in to break it up. Redd walked back in the house laughing.

"What the hell is so funny to you and what's wrong with your damn wife?" I was irritated that he thought this situation was funny. "She shouldn't even be here. What the hell does she have to do with what we are doing?"

"She's here because I say so, don't forget who running shit. You just make sure this shit jump off so you don't have to come up with the rest of my money. As for my wife, finding out that you still got it bad for her husband gets you a guaranteed ass whippin.'" Redd walked away from me as if the conversation was over. I swiftly followed behind.

"What do you mean found out I got it bad for you?" He smiled slyly and walked away. It looks like I wasn't getting an answer from him anytime soon. I walked to the back of the house to quickly regain myself. I checked my appearance in the mirror that hung at the end of the hallway. My face was still red from Queen's slap and now I had to go back into a room full woman and be the boss. I hated that bitch.

Walking back into the front room I could hear idle chit-chat from the girls. As soon as I stepped into the room an eerie silence fell across the room. Their smirking mouths and teasing eyes taunted me. Queen had confronted me in front of all these women and I knew it was just matter of time before one of them would try to test me too.

I decided to make the best of a bad situation and attempt to turn this around. I stepped up to speak. The first thing I did was make a mental note of the females that were now present. I saw Obsession sitting on Redd's lap in the back of the room. She was one to be watched.

"I'm sure all of you know exactly what you are here for. The key to this type of business is discretion. If you don't have it and you run your mouth, you need to walk towards the door now." I paused briefly. No one moved. "Secondly, your stripper names are out."

I could see rolling eyes and smacking lips but I didn't care. "So you need to think of a name to use when you are here, and anything with ending with isha, ika or quisha is out." I knew I was pissing them off, but again I didn't care.

"Please choose your name and before I leave to day I will approve it."

I went into my bag and pulled out a list I had made. "As far as money you keep forty percent of what you earn, the other sixty goes to the house." I was interrupted.

"What chu mean we only keep footy pressent?" I didn't even remember her name, Fantasy or something like that. I would have to give her a crash course in diction, cause this hoe couldn't talk. At least she didn't have to use her mouth for talking much. I walked towards her and stood within inches of her. I was so close I could feel the heat from her breath.

"I mean just what I said, you don't like it then move towards the door." I tilted my head, smiling sarcastically. We locked eyes. It was a game to me and I was going to win. I never broke eye contact. I wanted this bitch to try me. Redd needed to see results and fast and that wouldn't happen unless he was getting paid. I knew he would make the rest of what I owed him back, but the quicker he made it the faster he could release me from my debt.

"I can walk and tell everybody about what you are doing." She snapped back.

"Yeah you can, but we have our ways of dealing with snitches." She stared. I stared back. She had no idea that what I was saying was to merely intimidate her. She sucked her teeth and said nothing more.

I continued for the next thirty minutes uninterrupted as I laid down the ground rules of the house. If we were going to charge high dollar then they would want to get their money's worth. I walked the girls through house assigning each of them a bedroom. They could choose to sleep here or elsewhere at night, it didn't matter to me as long as they were here by noon everyday. I wasn't new to this, before I became Redd's other girl I was his highest paid girl and I could teach these girls a thing or two.

"Familiarize yourself with your room, rearrange things to your liking. I will return with Redd soon. Obsession walked with me. She moved very gracefully as if she were a dancer. I decided to give her the master bedroom. I knew she would be the star, and knowing that I would charge more for her meant I was willing to give a little more. In comparison to the other girls she was show stopping. I mean absolutely stunning. I don't know if she had extensions or if that was her real hair. Either way, she wore it well. We reached the master bedroom.

"This is going to be your bedroom." I opened the door revealing the room. There was a king sized bed with a pillow top mattress in the center of the room. She turned to me and smiled. I could tell she was pleased. I lifted my notepad so I could start to write.

"What name will you be using?"

"My middle name, Michelle." I smiled at her pleased. I didn't have to do a lot of explaining to her. She knew the rules of the game and was willing to play her part.

"Can I ask you something?"

"Sure you can." I was a bit apprehensive.

"What's the deal with you and Redd's wife? I thought you were his wife, until she introduced herself." Michelle gazed at me, waiting on a response.

"That's a story for another time and another place." I left the room to find Redd. I didn't care to go into the details of my sordid past. It was better left where it was and that was in the past.

***

*I waited outside of the courtroom for Trent. I left work early in hopes of surprising him for dinner. Normally in any relationship, it was all about me, but I wanted to do special things for him. Maybe somehow I felt guilty for the things I hid from him.*

*My intent wasn't to deceive. Well, that actually was exactly my intent, but in the midst of all of this I actually began to care about him. My plans were to make sure we never wanted for anything. I was just trying to give him a little push. The door to the courtroom swung open and Trent emerged. I stood to greet him, embracing him once he was close enough.*

*"Hey baby, I thought that I would be done but I'm not. Go ahead and go." He kissed me on my cheek and headed back towards the courtroom doors. Undoubtedly he had to do more work for the lead attorney.*

*As I was walking back I noticed Mr. Smith behind me. I'm sure he was watching my ass and I felt as if he was following me. I stopped and stood still.*

*"Why are you following me?"*

*"I'm not following you." He was beat red. I'm sure I make him uncomfortable, among other things.*

"Sure you are and it's a good thing I slowed down old guy. You know you can't keep up with me." I smiled slightly licking my lips to tease him. He watched me as I spoke, staring lustfully at me, unable to conceal his desire.

"Oh, I can keep up with you little girl." This is the first time he has ever tried to flirt back.

"Little girl? If I were a little girl maybe you could, but being a grown woman you--" "Why don't you have dinner with me. Your boyfriend will be working late tonight." He smiled. For an older guy, he was attractive. Not that I would ever consider anything serious with him, but it made what I was about to do a hell of a lot easier. He was being seduced and he didn't even know it.

I agreed to have dinner with him and was surprised. He wasn't boring, a little corny, but not boring. I sipped my wine and mindlessly listened as he talked. I don't know if it was being nervous or if he really talked that much.

My move to Houston was to change, to get away from those things I used to do and those people that wished me harm. But in some ways I hadn't changed. This was for a good cause, I justified. This was to change my life and Trent's, and I wouldn't have to do these type of things again.

---

# CHAPTER 8

---

I left Redd with his girls. I couldn't be in that house a moment longer. Who knows what freaky things he was dreaming up for them to do, especially Obsession, or Michelle I should say. Queen's slap was a brief dose of reality of the chaos I was dealing with. Redd had a way of getting into both my mind and my heart. I was falling so quickly I hadn't even stopped to remember all the reasons he was less than perfect for me.

He was the man that could make my toes curl. I needed to let go of the wild and crazy world that was Redd's life. Sure it was exciting but I was losing focus. The only reason I was helping him was to get away from him and stop him from destroying my life.

I parked my car in the parking garage across from Trent's firm and headed to the security desk to sign in. I recognized the guard and spoke, making idle chit-chat as he printed out my visitor's badge. I boarded the elevator on my way to Trent's office.

Normally when I would surprise him for lunch he would smile with delight, stop what he was doing and go to lunch with me. His office door was closed as I approached. I paused, tapping faintly to signal my entrance.

"Hey baby." Before I could fully open the door I noticed Queen sitting on the edge of his desk with her legs crossed appearing to take notes. Now when we met her he couldn't even remember her name, now he was having her work with him side by side. I didn't like what I saw.

"Am I interrupting?" I asked, my unhappiness apparent.

"No. I'm surprised to see you here." Trent never moved from his desk. He didn't bother to take his eyes off of Queen.

"Well, I thought I'd surprise you and take you to lunch." My anger was rising. It's as if I wasn't even in the room.

"I can't today, I have two cases I'm working on, I won't be able to get away for lunch, you should have called and checked." Trent finally looked my way. He still never moved from his desk.

"I never had to call before." I stared at him with icy contempt. The fact that this was playing out in front of her was embarrassing and it took every ounce of control within me to keep me from shoving her ass off of that desk. She stared my way, smirking as if she had won some type of silent battle. Trent finally decided to rise from his spot.

"Let me walk you out." Trent walked towards the door and held it open for me. Had I just been dismissed by my husband in front of that bitch? Was this payback for her being put out of the house that day by Redd?

He walked me back the elevator, kissed me on my cheek and left. The woman that reflected in the mirrored elevator doors looked troubled. At this point, I had no control of anything. Redd did whatever he pleased, my marriage, even though everything I felt I was doing was to save it, was spiraling out of control and half the time I didn't recognize my own damn reflection. A familiar voice startled me back to reality.

"Hello, Mrs. Jamison."

"Hi, how are you?" This was a conversation I didn't care to have. I didn't feel like being nice or sociable just because this was Trent's boss. Before a lengthy conversation could get started I was saved by the opening elevator doors. A look of disappointed washed over his face as I left him there to converse with himself.

I made it back to my car and contemplated my next move. I watched as countless people left the building for lunch. Could I really be hurt that my husband didn't want to have lunch with me? I was the one that was cheating on him with Redd every chance I got. I had to stop this affair with him, it's gotta be strictly business. I needed to get my life back. I didn't want to be Dominque. I enjoyed being Kyra. I enjoyed my lifestyle and I loved my husband.

Just as I started my car and was about to pull off. I noticed Trent leaving his office and he was not alone. Queen followed closely as they moved towards his car and got in. He was so busy he couldn't have lunch with me, yet he could take time out to have lunch with her. I knew what this was. Queen was out to destroy my life, literally and I refused to sit by and watch her do so. I picked up my cell phone and dialed a number I hadn't dialed in years.

"Jacob, it's Kyra." I hated having to come to him. I know what he will ask for.

"Kyra, you were just too busy to talk to me, weren't you? It was if I recall, Mr. Smith when you just saw me. You wouldn't even bother to look me in the eye. Now we are on first name basis again." He gloated for a moment but I knew how to quiet that down.

"Jacob, please stop. I need a favor from you." My patience was very short.

"What will I get for it?"

"Confidentiality. I won't run my mouth about things that could leave you with only half of what you've worked for."

"What is it?" He sounded defeated.

"Currently Trent has a paralegal working for him, Queen Richardson. I want her placed with another attorney."

"Queen is no longer a paralegal, she was promoted to an executive assistant job. Trent requested her. My hands are tied on that matter." I could hear him smirking through the phone. He was enjoying this.

"What do you mean your hands or tied? It's your firm." My words were dripping with anger.

"Yes, it's my firm and your husband is a partner in this firm, you do remember that. I'm sure you do as hard as you campaigned for it." His voice had transitioned from defeat to victory in a matter of moments. He knew he now had the upper hand and that his inside information was a blow to my ego.

"Bye, Jacob" I was done for now but this won't be the last. I had no idea Queen was now his executive assistant. I knew that job came with better pay and benefits, I just hoped one of the benefits wasn't my husband.

***

*Trent sat silently on my sofa as I prepared dinner for us. I watched him from the kitchen trying to decide if this was something that I wanted. I think I wanted him. I felt that he would change my life and possibly for the better. Together the possibilities were endless. It had been almost six months of us dating.*

*I knew he didn't have a lot of money but he always seemed to be able to surprise me and shower me with things. My money was diminishing quickly. Working at a bank I did learn the ins and outs of savings and CDs. I had money, but that was my in case I had to run money.*

*If I had to move and fast I would have something to start over with. Trent and I still hadn't had sex. I was trying to make a new start with him so I told him I was celibate and didn't want to rush things. I wanted to be one of those girls who didn't easily give it away. I felt like Kyra was that type of girl.*

*We sat down for dinner at the table and talked about things that didn't matter to me. I was tired of working and all I could think about was getting him the salary he needed to support me. I can't say that I was in love with him, but I hoped to love him one day. I placed my fork down and walked toward Trent. With each step I undid a button on my shirt. He watched* in silence as I moved towards him.

I let my clothes fall to the floor and began to dance for him. He never moved from his spot. His eyes were glued to my body. I led him to the bedroom and began to undress him. I could tell he thoroughly enjoyed it.

Suddenly I felt Trent's embrace tighten as he took control. This surprised me about him. He turned me over so that he was now on top. His stare was intense. He kissed my neck and ears. My body responded to him. Tiny chills ran up and down my spine as he showed me the real meaning of foreplay. I've had sex before, but this felt different.

"Let me make love to you." I surrendered to his control. He touched me in the emotional places that had been neglected for years. Moving in and out of me he took my body, kissing me as we explored one another. His pace was nice and slow, each stroke deeper than the first.

"I love you Kyra," he whispered in my ear.

Redd never told me he loved me, never took the time to kiss me like this. Redd and I had passion, maybe what we didn't have was love. I had given him all of me. Now it was time to let that go and allow myself to love Trent.

# CHAPTER 9

**M**y mind raced with thoughts of my husband and Queen. I knew she had to be trying to get back at me. My attempt to have her reassigned failed. I could go toe to toe with Jacob but I decided against it. I would save that threat for another day. My first thought was to follow Trent but I decided against it. Instead, I decided to go home and take some time for myself. Anxiety consumed me and I hadn't slept much since that day at the benefit when Queen and Redd walked back into my life.

I walked into my home feeling confused. After seeing the obvious attraction Trent had to Queen I felt conflicted. I know the things I've done are far from right, but it's entirely different when you see the person you love admiring someone else. I had never had to worry about Trent being attracted to anyone else, at least if he was I never knew about it. I walked towards our bedroom and noticed Trent's clothes sitting on the chaise.

I gathered them to take them to the cleaners. As I picked up his clothes I could smell the vague scent of perfume. I sniffed, but I was unable to identify the scent. This just confirmed what I already knew. There was another woman and I was willing to bet it was Queen. I threw the clothes down, disgusted, and decided to take a shower.

I went to the bathroom to turn on the hot water, undressed and stepped in. Showers always seemed to take the pain away. The water to washed over me and took the pain I felt down the drain with it. Somewhere in the back of my mind a voice screamed that I was doing the same thing, so how could I be mad, but I was. My association with Redd was business and it protected my husband as well as myself.

I stepped out of the shower and grabbed a towel. When I walked out of the bathroom Redd was sitting on my bed. It was time to end this nonsense with him. I know I wanted my marriage and I had to stop.

"What the hell are you doing in my house?" He acted as if the bed belonged to him.

"Why the hell did you leave the spot?" His eyes were dead pools that stared at me, empty of any emotion. If he ever felt anything for me I couldn't see it now.

"Because you and your wife are got damn lunatics." My heart rate began to skip. I don't know how much craziness I can take.

"I'm going to excuse you saying that. You get dressed and get your ass back to that house. We starting up tomorrow. We already have clients on the books."

"Just leave Redd and give me time to myself."

"You've had twelve years to yourself on my dime. I told yo ass it was payback time." Redd walked out of the house and slammed the door. I weighed my options and decided to return back to the house.When I got there the girls were all sitting in the dining area.

"What's going on?'

"We're installing cameras." Michelle was the first to speak. I nodded and walked past them to the study which was set up as an office. All of the surveillance screens had been setup in the office. As each of the room cameras became operable I could see the bedrooms. I looked around the house. I had helped Redd build his establishment better than he could ever hope for.

This was ten times better than anything he had going on when he was set up in New Orleans. I watched as the girls went back to their rooms. They all began to do meaningless task, all except for Michelle. She appeared to be studying. A stripper with a book wasn't an everyday sight.

Something about that intrigued me. I wanted to know more. I knocked on her door, this was my best attempt at not being rude I mean this was technically my house. After a few seconds she opened it.

"Hey Dominique, what's up?" I almost corrected her and told her my name was Kyra but remembered I told them to call me that. They would never know who Kyra Jamison was.

"Nothing, I stopped by to make sure you had everything you needed for tomorrow."

"Everything is great. I'm just doing a little studying. Let me ask you something. Even when we are not working is it okay if we stay here."

" I don't mind but you may want to just clear it with Redd." I knew Redd well enough to know if he didn't feel like he was in charge he would go crazy.

"Sure I'll do that. So you ever gonna tell me the story between the two of you. You guys looked like you were together the night I met you." She was nosey. I came to ask the questions not answer them. I didn't even acknowledge that she had asked the question.

"So you are studying, what are you studying?" I looked over her shoulder trying to get a glimpse of what she was reading.

"I'm in school, this whole stripper hoe thing

is temporary. Honestly, I am just doing it to get by. It's a lot easier to shake my ass for major tips than to work an every day nine to five for minimum wage. I'm getting a degree in Forensic Accounting, this is the last year so I'm almost done with the self exploitation."

What the fuck was forensic accounting?

"Well, I was just making sure everything was good," I said before walking off. I was done for the day no matter what Redd said. I grabbed my purse and walked out the door. I did need time to myself. I felt that I was so far in that I wouldn't be able to see myself out.

*** 

*Mr. Smith sat at the edge of my bed and stared at me. I assumed this was his sexy face. His pale white skin appeared blue in certain places as the moonlight from the open window danced across his skin.   He was in no way prepared for what would happen in his life next. I strained to see the tiny camcorder on my tv stand in the dimly lit room. I slyly reached over to press a button to make sure it started to record.*

*"Why don't we turn some light on, I want to be able to see you as you make love to me." I couldn't care less about making love to this dude, I just wanted to make sure that the camera could see everything that was happening. He just smiled and moved towards me. He grabbed my toes and began to slowly suck each one.*

*He then traced kisses up my thigh and began to taste me. I have to say I was surprised that he wasn't horrible at what he was doing. I pushed my hips towards him to allow him to penetrate me deeper. After twenty minutes he was done and his sweaty body fell against mine.*

*I was relieved when he finally left. I hurried to watch the tape and then made copies of it. I made sure to choose positions where his face would be fully visible. I placed a copy in a brown envelope that I would deliver to him first thing tomorrow morning. I washed my body,* called Trent and then fell asleep.

The next day I walked into the office with a huge smile on my face and went straight to Mr. Smith's office. He looked at me with surprise. It was one thing to fuck me, it was another for me to show up and barge into his office as if I knew him.

I placed the envelope in front of him. "It's everything we did last night." I laughed. He wore a look of disbelief on his face. "Yes, I recorded it. It's insurance. I need you to give Trent a helping hand. He's done with law school, now make him a lawyer and pull him out of that pen of junior associates. Give him real work, real pay." Everything became silent.

"And if I don't, you do know that blackmail is against the law. And I'm a lawyer." He answered smugly as if that was supposed to scare me.

"Did you know fucking a black girl could get you divorced? And for a guy like you, divorce can lead to losing a lot of money as well as reputation when I leak this tape to the press. I don't have anything to lose, you on the other hand, have everything to lose."

"What about Trent, you could lose him."

"I won't, cause you ain't gonna tell. I'm not asking for you to make him partner, he will do that on his own. But you will give him a chance and a salary double what he's making now." I stood before him, silent, but my eyes spoke volumes.

"Why would you do this?" His eyes were pleading with me to stop.

"It's to ensure my future. You have forty-eight hours to make your decision." I turned around and walked out of his office and headed to the lower level where Trent's cubicle was. I suspected after today, Trent would be moving out and into an office of his own.

# CHAPTER 10

Money flowed like the currents of the Mississippi. With the passing months, Redd's spot went from slow and boring to on and popping. I was amazed by the steady stream of patrons that were in and out of the doors of this place and with my help these men definitely got the most. It was top notch and you couldn't walk through those doors spending less than five hundred. A grand would get you a good time, but two stacks would get you nothing less than full service.

Redd had even set up a bar so to speak, you could get any desired drink or drug you wanted, at an extra cost I lifted my notepad so I could start to write. Discretion was the name of the game. A car rotated hourly bringing and taking customers back to their cars or offices. Because of the location, we didn't have to worry about nosey neighbors wondering what was going on. Our shit was together, and I knew with my help, Redd could be on another level.

I sat in the study with the many video monitors surrounding me. Redd was bringing in the money. He could make ten thousand a day now that things had started really moving. Most of the men that came through the doors were white, many of them with high profile jobs and a lot of money to throw around. I was swiftly paying off my debt and couldn't wait to be free of this. I wanted to go back to my safety net. I wanted to go back to the simplicity of my life.

My old life seemed so far away from me now. Trent spent more and more time away from home. He never seemed to be in his office when I called and the strange scent that I smelled on his clothes was now familiar because he often smelled of the floral fragrance when he came home. The scent of that same fragrance hit my nostrils. I turned to see Queen standing behind me.

"What?" I wanted to keep my distance from this nut. I didn't want to have a fight every time I saw her.

"Are you still fucking my husband?" I turned back around to the computer and continued entering appointment logs.

"Are you fucking mine?"

"Hoe, I'm about to fuck your whole life." Queen turned around and left the room. Good. I would much rather be by myself than to have her for company.

I gazed at the monitors. I looked towards the door to make sure Queen had closed it. The monitors were set up to make sure everything went as it should. None of the girls were allowed to touch the money. All money came to the house first and then the girls got their percentage at the end of the night. They did so well here most of them had quit stripping and made this their full time.

I recognized him from the back first. My eyes were glued to the screens. The sensual cockiness of his walk caught my attention. Its familiarity shocked me and when he turned to face the bedroom camera my heart burst. I couldn't understand how this happened. I watched the train wreck as it happened before me. I stared as he touched her, the ways that he had once touched me.

Tears streamed from my eyes. I didn't know what my next move should be. I know I wanted to run to the room and tell her to get the hell off of my husband. He reached for what appeared to be marijuana, lit it and puffed as she rode him. The man I saw before me was a complete stranger. I thought of the compromising positions I've put myself into all in the name of protecting him from my history.

I became again what I despised in order to keep his resume impeccable and his reputation top notch. My actions not only protected me but him as well. All the guilt and yo-yo feelings I was having about sleeping with Redd and he's probably been doing things like this all along.

I decided not to move. I would confront him later. I didn't want the embarrassment of the girls knowing my husband was a paying customer. I pressed record to create a video of what was taking place. He would have no way of denying it. I decided tonight we would be coming clean. They took what appeared to be a break. I picked up my cell phone and dialed his number, curious as to what he was going to say.

"Hey baby, are you busy?" I was surprised he answered.

"A little, working on a case, I will probably be working late tonight." Before I could say another word the phone went dead and my eyes told me why. Another girl had entered the room and now sat across his lap as the other sat on his face. I was disgusted by these actions and knew I didn't want to be anywhere near him. If I hadn't been so caught up with Redd I probably would have seen all of this coming.

Unable to watch anymore I left. I went directly home where I played the video with half of his sexual interlude on the big screen. I wanted to make sure that it was playing when he walked through the door. Even though I knew it had to be done, I wasn't prepared to have this conversation.

As I took a shower my mind wondered. I journeyed through the whys and hows of my circumstances. No one did this to me, I am a victim of my own actions and decisions. I took Redd's money. I was the one that decided to handle things my way instead of going to my husband with the truth. And I was the one that was blinded by the feeling of euphoria when with Redd, that I failed to see things happening in front of me. My secrets were coming full circle.

I heard him open the front door and then it closed. Footsteps paced the ceramic tile as he walked through the house, then I heard nothing. Finding my strength from somewhere, I moved towards the family room where I knew he would be. I stopped at the doorway as he watched the screen. He turned to face me as if he sensed my presence.

"What the hell is this?"

"Shouldn't I be asking you that?"

"So are you spying on me?" His eyes were pure venom as he watched me.

"No, but you are cheating on me I see." I watched Trent as he dropped his briefcase and smiled. He never said a word as he walked pass me. I can't say that I wasn't confused. Trent had always been so in love with me, enamored, I mean I was his trophy and now I felt more like a burden. My face became heated as I followed him out of the room.

"Trent, you hear me talking to you!"

"We don't want to talk about cheating. Every day you have somewhere to go. Every night you come in smelling of smoke and alcohol. I know you don't think I'm stupid. You've been fucking someone, so don't pretend you are innocent in everything." He stared at me. Removing his clothing unusually slow.

"You don't know what I've been doing cause you're too busy having sex with prostitutes. This is not us Trent." I was so upset with him that I could have slapped him.

"Isn't that all you are?"

I stood shocked, surprised that I had been called a whore by the man that I loved. Completely lost for words, my anger took control and began to steer my actions. My hands swung as I clawed at his face. He grabbed my hands mid-air and threw me towards the floor. Before I knew it he was on top of me. His eyes glowed with hatred, with anger so strong I feared him at this moment.

"You're my whore aren't you? I pay good money to fuck you, whenever I want. You're no different from those girls at that place, just how many men have had you for just the right price?" He finally released me from his hold as he moved off of me. I rolled into a fetal position, rendered immobile from the emotional bruises he had left me with.

"Trent, you can't mean that?" I pleaded for him to take back his words.

"Like hell I don't." He said and moved towards the bathroom door and locked himself inside.

I struggled to stand up. Both my ego and body were bruised by Trent. I didn't know what just happened or how my husband has lost all respect for me, but I had an idea. Just like other issues in my life, I believed Queen had set these wheels in motion.

***

*Everything had gone according to plan. Trent and I were planning our wedding. Trent had a great promotion, and was proving himself every day as one of the strongest attorneys in the firm. I had quit my job and moved in with him.*

*For the first time in my life, I felt things were going the way they should. It seemed that things in my life were finally easier. Being Kyra was the best thing that ever happened to me. As we worked out the guest list I told Trent the last lie I promised myself I would tell. I had to have a reason why I didn't have any family coming.*

*He wanted to know why my mother couldn't come and even offered to pay for the expenses for my family to come to the wedding. I knew I would have to think fast, so I did what I knew best. I let the lies to roll off my tongue as if they were pure truth.*

*"I just don't understand. Shouldn't some of your family want to be here? You never talk about them or anything."*

*My eyes filled with tears. "I don't have any family. I don't talk about them because my mom and sister both died in a house fire and I spent the remainder of my years in foster care." That was a lie, in fact, my mother still was in the hell hole I left her ass in and I hadn't heard from my sister in years. But I knew if I said they were dead he wouldn't question it.*

*"Baby, you never told me, I'm sorry" He held me in his arms as the fake tears streamed down my face.*

*"That's okay baby, your family will be here for us."*

*"The little family I have here yes, they will make it. I guess it will be mostly our closest friends then. Who comes doesn't matter, this is about us, it's about our union." He hugged me.*

*Life was what it was supposed to be. I finally felt satisfied that I wouldn't have to run from Redd anymore. Honestly, how could he find me? I think I hid well. He couldn't trace me by cell phone, by the car, I had and I definitely did not have the same name. Dominique was gone.*

*I lay silently against my husband to be as my cell phone vibrated against my leg. I didn't plan on answering it. I had rejected at least ten calls today from an unavailable number.*

*"Aren't you gonna get your phone."*

*"No, I'm enjoying my time with you too much." My answer seemed sufficient enough. He didn't bother to push me any further and I was thankful. My phone continued to ring as we sat in a comfortable silence. I discretely pushed*

*the side button on my iPhone to immediately silence my phone.*

*I didn't know who it was that was calling me, but I knew I didn't want to be found. There was no way after I've done so much that I would risk losing everything. I moved closer to Trent attempting to shake away the negative feelings that the consistently ringing phone gave me. I no longer wanted to deal with being Dominque.*

*I was Kyra now, I was soon to be a lawyer's wife, I had a career, and I would have a family. I was everything that Dominque could never be. I felt the phone vibrate one last time against my leg.*

*"Baby, give me a second, I gotta go to the bathroom." Trent looked up from the book he was reading and shook his head okay.*

*"Kyra, you don't need my permission to use the bathroom." He laughed, I guess finding it absurd that I needed to announce my journey to the toilet.*

*"I know babe." I headed towards the bathroom and closed the door. I reached into the back pocket of my jeans to retrieve my phone and firmly pressed my fingerprint against the home key to unlock it. I had a total of 20 missed calls and they were all private. I hit the voicemail icon, brought the phone up to my*

*ear and began to listen.*

*I instantly recognized the deep voice on the other line. Anger dripped from his words and it was a side I had never seen of him before. Sharp breaths escaped between the vicious verbal daggers he threw at me. It seems his proper tone and ivy league vocabulary had escaped him.*

*The more I think about it Kyra, the more pissed off I become. Do you really think you can blackmail me? Bitch please I invented blackmail. Just know you have fired the first shot! It's about to be a war.*

*For a brief moment, I looked at my phone in disbelief. Could this man actually be serious? I tapped the trash icon with the tip of my thumb, discarding, message and any memory of Jacob's threat. What could he do to me? He didn't even really know who I was.*

# CHAPTER 11

The last words my husband spoke to me played over in my head. I was unsure of how to take what was happening. My life had literally begun to fall apart and I felt powerless to do anything about it. Hurt and anger engulfed me as I waited for Trent to come out of the bathroom. I watched the door, seething with venomous fury. Last night Trent arrogantly walked away from me and refused my pleas for attention.

I honestly just wanted to get to the bottom of what was happening, I am fighting so hard for this marriage, compromising who I am now for who I was before, all to protect him from my past.

"Treeeeeent!" I screamed to the top of my lungs. I refused to be ignored. When it came to Trent I felt guilt and blame for anything that ever went wrong in our marriage. I took on all of the burden and stress of the relationship in order to make him happy. In order to make him into the best possible version of himself, I was willing to sacrifice pieces of me.

I jumped up from the seat I was rooted in all night. Trent was in the bathroom far too long. I moved swiftly towards the door determined to break it down if I had too. My satin robe flowed behind me as I created my own tornado of anger. One after the other my small fist banged against the door, demanding to be heard.

Just as I went to hit the door for the millionth time it swung open. Trent was standing before me fully dressed. His lips curled and twisted with annoyance as he stared at me waiting for me to speak.

"Where are you going Trent? We need to talk."

"I don't have anything to say to you, I thought I made that clear."

"This is our marriage, it deserves a conversation." My eyes pleaded with him. I was silently begging him to find some form of the compassion like he used to feel for me. He lowered his gaze for a brief moment, breaking our intense eye contact. For a moment I saw a flicker of an emotion other than anger from him and then just as quickly as it came, it was gone.

He pushed past me and walked into our bedroom. I followed as fast as my feet could carry me. He reached for a bag sitting on the foot of the bed. I squinted my eyes in complete disbelief; it was my luggage that he was lifting.

"What are you doing with my bag?" Was he

eaving?

"I'm helping you with your things so you can get out." The look in his eyes scared me. He spoke evenly, with a cool tone that said that he didn't really care. Tears filled my eyes.

"I'm not going anywhere!"

"Yeah, you're getting the fuck out now, I'm done." His words said he was serious. I was hurting; he was angry, neither one of us were thinking in our right mind. I had to persuade him to talk to me. I planted my feet into the ground as if to say, "I'm not going." The standoff had begun.

I didn't need to speak any words at this point to let him know I wasn't leaving. I believed I had sacrificed all that I am not only for my survival but the survival of this relationship; he wasn't going to just toss me out like trash.

"I'm not leaving."

"Yeah, you are." Trent grabbed the packed bag, dragged it to the front door and then tossed it out. The force with which he moved terrified me. I squinted my eyes attempting to recognize the man that I had once knew. This was a stranger to me. Still refusing to leave my home, our home, I stood firmly, willing him to talk to me so that we could work whatever issue we had out.

I was baffled by all that was happening around me, it seemed that my life was completely turned upside down. One moment this man was completely in love with me the next moment it seems as if he hates me.

The sound of Trent's booming voice snapped me back into reality. Before I could focus on what he was saying I felt the firm grasp of his arms wrapping around my body. He forcefully pulled me from my spot.

"Let me go!" I kicked and pushed attempting to get away from him. My legs desperately and unsuccessfully fought aimlessly against the air. The robe that covered my semi-nude body began to slip away, exposing my bare skin just as my husband's actions were exposing the callousness of his heart.

I felt a surge of pain shoot through my body as my ass met the hard cement driveway. He was throwing me out like garbage, and worst of all hadn't so much as given me an explanation as to why.

"Trent, what is happening, what did I do to you to deserve this? I'm not the one who was caught cheating, I'm not the one that obviously has a thing for my assistant, and I'm not the one that refused to talk about it. "

Last night I walked through the doors of my home fully prepared to come clean, I wanted to put everything on the table and move forward with the life and image I had worked so hard to achieve.

"You know exactly what you've done, and for you to try to sit here and play innocent disgusts me. Did you think I was stupid? Did you think I would never find out who you really are?"

"Trent I'm exactly who you know me to be?" Even though I didn't fully believe the words, I was convinced they had enough truth in them to speak them now.

"I don't know who you are, but I do know this, Kyra Williams did not exist before 2005. There are no school records, no birth records, and no established credit, absolutely nothing. Kyra Williams-Jamison does not exist." Before I could respond, the door abruptly slammed shut.

***

*The day that some women dream about was finally here. Dominique was not one of those women, but Kyra was. I turned in the full-size mirror completely enamored with my own reflection. I would have never had this type of life in Louisiana. Back home I was someone different, someone who didn't get diamond rings and wedding gowns. I was the one men used to fulfill their fantasies, but today all that had changed.*

*I opted for a simple ceremony; something small and intimate is how I explained it to Trent. It would be just us, I would walk down the aisle to meet him, he would take my hand and we would exchange vows. I limited the guest list to just his immediate family and a few friends. I could never let him know it was because I had no contact with my family and friends.*

*He could never know that I had stolen from my married drug-dealing boyfriend after receiving a death threat from his psychotic wife. No, small and intimate sounded much better.*

*A light knock at the door interrupted my thoughts. I walked to the door to unlock it. I guessed it was probably someone from the venue to let me know that it was time. I grasped the knob to open the door. I put on my "I'm so excited to be getting married" smile because I was expecting to see the little white lady* who had led me to this room, my smile quickly vanished.

"Jacob." He stared at me, his smooth porcelain colored skin slightly tanned from the summer sun.

"Kyra." He pushed his way into my room.

"What do you want?"

"Here," He handed me a pastel pink envelop with the words, on your wedding day printed on them. I ran my finger in the corner to rip it open and pulled out the contents. Reading the front of the card, it seemed like no more than a kind gesture to a bride on her wedding day, but I knew Jacob a little better than that. The messages he has been leaving me say that this is not a friendly meeting.

Inside the card were pieces of paper. I squinted my eyes as I read the paper. I could feel the blood drain from my face, as my past and my present collided.

"What is this?" I questioned.

"It's my insurance plan."

"Jacob I - -".

"I'll talk. You just listen. This is my insurance plan! You can either play the game my way, and I'll stop looking or do it your way and watch me show you how blackmail really works."

"I don't know what this is." My tongue tripped over the words. I was so nervous I was stuttering. I knew exactly what it was. I could read very well. It was a background check on Kyra Williams. It said everything I had paid thousands of dollars for, but the thing that made my heart beat a million beats per minute was the picture he had included inside of the card. It was a mugshot.

"Yeah, you know what it is. You thought you could play with me little girl? I didn't get to where I am today by playing by the rules. You should have done your homework before you decided to blackmail me. I don't know who Dominque Simoneaux is, at the moment I don't care, but try to blackmail me again and everybody will find out. Police included."

He walked over to me and lifted the many layers of my dress. I didn't know what to do, this man how somehow gotten the upper hand in my own game. My mind raced trying to come up with my next move. I felt his hands slide between my thighs and gently brush against me.

"We're not done until I say it's done. You want your husband to keep climbing, then we do things the way I want, when I want. As long as you keep my secret, I'll keep yours." He pulled away from me and without saying another word, left.

# CHAPTER 12

How the hell had he found out? How much did he really know? Questions swirled around in my head as I drove aimlessly. My heart was still racing thinking about the coldness Trent displayed. In this very moment, I wanted to be just as cold and cruel to him as he was being to me. It was obvious that I am not the only one with secrets. It was becoming more and more apparent to me that Trent harbored probably just a many secrets as I did, maybe even more.

The man I just saw was not the man that I married. Trent was the man I thought would never hurt me. When I found him he was so different from what I was used to. He put me first, I felt special, like he had eyes for only me and would protect my heart by any means necessary, and I, in turn, was willing to do any and everything to make our marriage and him successful.

My eyes were dry from shedding so many tears. I had no more; the only emotion I could feel was anger. Anger that I had gone to such lengths to protect a man who in the end only saw me the same way as any other man had. A possession. I felt alone, and the one thing I didn't want to be right now was alone.

I picked up my phone to call Redd. I didn't know what I thought he could do for me but whatever it was had to be better than feeling the way I did. Anything was better than this empty, dark feeling that was starting to take control of me. I would deal with Trent, but I had to clear my mind to do so.  I never thought I would be confiding in Redd ever again, but as I drove he was the only one I could think of that I could talk to.

"Hey, where are you?"

"On my way to the house, what's up?"

"I'll meet you there." I disconnected the call. I didn't want to talk on the phone, but I did need to see him. Before all of this, before Queen found out, before I robbed him, when we were back home and just us, he actually did make a good friend. I knew I could expose all of me to him because he knew all of my flaws, and he would give me his honest opinion about what I should do next.

I pulled my car into the private driveway and parked. I grabbed the rearview mirror and looked at myself. My eyes were puffy and red from my endless crying, my hair which was usually always in place was messy and disheveled; I was a hot mess.  I grabbed my purse and attempted to somewhat put myself together. I didn't want any of those girls to see me like this. Once I felt satisfied that I was as together as I could be under the circumstances I got out of the car and went in.

It was unusually quiet in the house, but at the moment I didn't care to question it or even mind the silence. I welcomed it. It was early in the day so most of the ladies hadn't come in yet. This was the time Redd and I usually used to go over the books. I walked in and headed towards the master suite. I knocked gently before entering making sure that the room was empty. Once I entered I headed towards the master bath, water always worked wonders to clear my mind.

Piece by piece I began to remove my clothing until I was completely naked. I moved towards the oversized tub, slid in and started a warm flow of water that washed over me. I felt safe submerged in the warm pool of water. I stared at the walls, at first void of all emotion, and then the dam broke. Everything I had been running from had rushed in from every end. I was engulfed in turmoil, nothing was right in my life. The more I struggled to hold on to control, the more I began to lose control.

"Kyra?" Her sugary sweet tone broke through my thoughts of self-pity. I turned to face Michelle. My vulnerability showed. "What's wrong?"

"Nothing." My voice was nearly gone from all the yelling I had done with Trent.

"I can tell there is something, but you don't have to talk about it."

Good, I thought to myself as I turned away from her, before increasing the intensity of the jets on the tub. I closed my eyes and sank deeper, hoping she would take the hint to go away.

"What are you doing?" The unexpected movement of the water startled me. I sat straight up and stared at Michelle sitting across from me.

"I'm taking your mind off of whatever is bothering you." I'm not sure what made her think that me soaking in this bathtub was an open invitation. I pulled my legs closer to my body, uncomfortable with being in the tub with her. I know things had gotten out of hand with her and Redd at the club, but it wasn't that type of party.

That was a one-time thing that I did not plan on repeating. The further I pulled away the closer she seemed to get to me. I was in the furthest corner of the tub, there was nowhere else for me to move. She didn't say any words, just stared at me, intensely, instead of looking at me she looked through me. Her hands moved up my legs as she pulled me into her. I could feel the warmth of her body against me.

My mind argued with my body, I wanted her to stop, but then I didn't. I wanted to feel something else other than the emotions and pain that had taken permanent residence in my heart. If I felt something physical, I wouldn't think about raging emotions.

I began to let down my guard. My legs relaxed and slightly parted as she found her way between them.

"Uh-hmmm!" The clearing of his throat was an obvious but immediate attention getter. "I thought you wanted to talk about something." He smirked as he watched me uncomfortably lift myself from the tub.

"I do want to talk." My cheeks were red with embarrassment. I didn't want to be caught in such a compromising position by Redd. I would never live it down.

"Why you running? It's nothing I've never seen before."

I pushed pass him and headed into the bedroom. I stumbled as I slipped my clothes on but soon realized I had much bigger problems to worry about than Redd finding me butt naked in the bathtub with her. I finished dressing and turned to face both of them. Michelle hadn't spoken a word. She carelessly stood naked in the room as if nothing was happening. In her world it seemed to just be her. Maybe she was waiting for a repeat of the night we had met her.

"We need to talk." My eyebrows raised

slightly to give him the signal that this was an important conversation. He instantly understood. That's the one thing about Redd and I, we never really needed words; we always had so many other ways of communicating.

"Michelle, you gonna have to table your little lesbian love affair, we got business." She exited the room, not bothering to even put her clothes on before. Redd walked behind her and closed the door.

"Now, what is so important?"

"He knows."

"He knoooooows what? And who the hell is he?"

"Trent."

"Oh, your punk ass husband."

"I'm serious." I needed him to take this seriously, depending on what he knows we could go down for all this shit we are doing. Anger began to build within me. I was doing all this so he didn't find out who I was and he knows that I am not who I am.

"So what your husband got to do with me?"

"He knows something Redd, he was in here yesterday. When I went home to confront him about it he flipped the hell out. Grabbed my ass, through me to the floor called me his whore and choked me until I almost passed out, Then…"

"What the fuck you say he did? Choked you? And that nigga still breathing?"

"Wait, then this morning he threw my ass out the door."

As I recounted everything that had happened, I could see it was finally sinking in. Redd was finally catching up.

"How did he find out?"

"I don't know, but if I had to guess I would say he was tipped off by your dumb ass wife. I don't even know how much he knows. I gotta figure that out first. He was pissed Redd." I shook my head as if I could dislodge the thoughts of what had just happened.

"He just said that he knew my name wasn't really Kyra."

"It doesn't seem like he knows shit."

"It sounds like he knows enough."

***

*Three months have passed since my wedding day and the day Jacob showed me a completely different side of himself. I couldn't figure out what his angle was and I didn't know how to contain the information that I knew he had on me. Right now even though everything was peaceful I was smart enough to understand that he had the upper hand.*

*An overwhelming wave of anxiety passed over me. Every piece of my well-designed life had been carefully placed liked the blocks of a Jenga tower. It looked good, but one wrong move and it would topple over into ruins. I had to think of a way to get out of the conundrum I found myself in.*

*When I met Jacob I thought I had completely read him. He looked like an easy mark that I could control and he had played along well. I wondered just how long Jacob had known I wasn't really who I pretended to be.*

*I looked around our apartment. I liked my life. It felt nice not to have to worry about the threats that came from leading the street life. With Trent, I had found some sort of normalcy and a place to hide in plain sight. With my "tips" I gave to the NOPD I felt certain I no longer had to fear Redd coming after me, at least for now. My only real threat was coming from the very person I thought I had control over.*

*I was drowning in nervousness. Every single nerve ending tingled with anticipation. I couldn't live like this. I knew what I had to do. Rushing to get dressed I ran to my bedroom. My first mind told me to get sexy, but I believed I was far beyond that with Jacob. I seriously doubt given everything that has happened that my sex appeal would do anything. I slipped on my shoes and headed towards the car.*

*Once I arrived at the office I went to the lower level. This is the area we always met in, it was restricted and could only be accessed with a key card, this way we were less likely to be seen together. I used the one Jacob gave me when I thought I was seducing him. I sat in the parking garage trying to figure out the right words to say.*

*I just needed assurance that we could keep it between us. From what Jacob has been showing me it would be best to appeal to his ego rather than anything else. How in the world had I missed that? My body fell into my plush leather seat as I sat in my car contemplating whether to send a message asking Jacob to meet me downstairs.*

*Just as I found the courage to send that text, I noticed a black SUV pull into the garage. Normally this wouldn't seem strange, but it's the way it crept through the garage. The car moved slowly through the dim area and rolled to a stop right as it reached the elevator.*

*I sat forward to get a better look. The man that exited the rear driver's side door was tall and muscular; he looked a lot like Trent from behind but he was taller and darker. I couldn't make out his face, he never moved beyond the shadows of the garage.*

*Not wanting to be seen, I sank as deep as I could into the driver's seat without obstructing my view. The light from my screen illuminated the inside of the car. I quickly exited the unsent message and opened my camera. I dimmed the screen as much as possible and began to record the scene before me. I eyed the man up and down.*

*It wasn't Trent, this man was older but just as handsome. His skin was the smooth texture of milk chocolate. His custom tailored suit fit his firmly toned body perfectly. I watched as he walked along the side of the SUV and stood next to the elevator. He eyed his watch impatiently as if he was waiting for someone.*

*The dim light in the waiting area for the elevator washed across him but I didn't recognize the man. Something about his features seemed familiar. I struggled to attempt to connect the pieces of my memory. Did I know this man or was my mind just playing tricks on me? I could feel the chaotic bumping of my heart as I watched.*

The shuffling sound of the elevator doors opening invaded the silence in the parking garage. Jacob exited and greeted the man. I could barely hear but I could tell that these two were very familiar with one another. It didn't make any sense to me. As if on cue the driver got out of the car and opened the back. As the door went up, I saw what I thought was a body flailing around.

My heartbeat quickened. My mind rushed to make sense of what I was seeing. I wasn't new to any of this, and what I saw looked like someone who was about to meet their end. The driver grabbed the man inside and threw him to the ground. He struggled to gain his balance as the driver stood him up. His hands were tied to his sides and his mouth was taped. The driver reached and snatched the tape from his mouth before retreating back to his spot in the car.

The man stood defeated. His slumped composure told me he had no hope of things going his way. Jacob moved towards him and without so much as saying a word, he punches the hell out of him. The sound of flesh hitting flesh echoed through the garage.

"Didn't I fucking tell you if I ever caught you stealing, you would pay with your life?" Jacob's snow white skinned reddened as he spoke through clenched teeth. I don't think I had ever seen him this angry. Until the day of my wedding, I would have never thought that he could so much as get angry. But clearly he could. The man didn't answer only looked at him with I could only guess was pleading eyes.

"Where's my money?" The man moved closer. His body language was menacing. The closer he moved to the man the faster my pulse quickened. I would not want to be this man. He had broken the number one rule. He got caught.

"I have it, I'll give it back, please." The man in the suit tapped on the back a truck and the driver got out of the car again, this time carrying an iPad. He handed it to Jacob. After a moment of pressing and swiping he spoke.

"Give me the passwords," he demanded.

"G-g-e-t-t-h-A-t-$_4-M-e," The man said through frightened gasps. I watched as Jacob swiped and tapped some more before handing it back to the driver who stood silently to the side.

"It's done, all of your money will be back in its rightful place by the close of business today." He turned to look at the man who was now shaking. "Thank you." A sinister smile spread across Jacob's face and then disappeared.

"Don't make a mess in my garage." He said to the driver and then pressed the button to enter the elevator. I wanted to look away but I couldn't. I sat in paralyzed, horrified as the driver turned into a hitman. He grabbed something from the truck, wrapped it around the bound man's neck, and squeezed until his body went limp.

I sat waiting in my car afraid to move as I watched him throw the body in the car and leave. I didn't want to follow them out so I sat and waited for what I thought would be enough time for them to have left.

I hit end on the recorded and quickly scrolled to my unsent message. I erased it; thankful I hadn't sent it. After what I just saw I wanted no trace of me being here and I no longer thought it would be a good idea to mess with Jacob, but I knew this recording would buy me a bit of insurance in case he came for me.

I hoped I never had to use it but if he exposed me it would be mutually assured destruction, I would take his ass down with me. I didn't understand everything that had happened but I understood one thing, Jacob wasn't exactly who he claimed to be. My best bet would be to lay low, be a good little wife and not provoke him to spill my secret.

# CHAPTER 13

The warmth of Redd's body wrapped around me like a child's favorite blankey. I felt safe in this very moment. The sun peaked through the semi-closed blinds creating an ethereal glow throughout the room. If I had it my way I wouldn't move from this spot. Lying next to him reminded me of the times I had run away from, things at times somehow seemed perfect, but always fleeting. The bed gently moved as Redd began to wake and turn to face me.

"Good morning," He lifted his head, his eyes still half closed.

"Hey."

"What?" His partially opened eyes were twisted in confusion, or maybe it was annoyance.

"Everything Redd, what the hell am I going to do about Trent?"

Redd sat up in the bed now fully awake. His face was twisted in annoyance. His expression told me he didn't understand how my life seemed to be crumbling around me.

"Do nothing about that nothing ass nigga."

"That nothing ass nigga is still my husband, all of my money everything is tied up in joint accounts. I gave you everything I had separately to clear my debt with you. Remember!" I moved to the side of the bed. I was annoyed that he didn't seem to understand what was happening.

"Look Dominque, fuck that nigga. We got the spot, we making money. You don't need him. Besides, it's always gonna be mine anyway." Redd walked over to the side of the bed and pushed me back against the plush mattress. My body immediately reacted as he began to kiss me against my neck. Slowly he moved down, using his tongue to trace sensual lines leading to my nipples.

My back arched as his touch commanded my body. As Redd's hands traveled the length of my body, my thoughts of Trent slipped away.

"Damn." Redd shouted reaching for his phone. I sat up to peek at the screen.

*My Queen*

I quickly read before he moved to answer. So much for my welcomed distraction. Queen seemed to be in the midst of everything. I watched as Redd left the room to speak to her in private. I assumed she was calling because he didn't come home last night. I began to put my clothes on and sat waiting for Redd. This again reminded me of our old times and our fleeting moments. Things always seemed perfect and then they weren't.

I shrugged my shoulders and proceeded to put on my shoes. It didn't matter figuring out things with Redd was further down on my list. Things would never really be different. As long as Queen is around we would always be in the exact same place.

"Where you going?"

"I gotta figure some stuff out."

"Look I told you, don't worry about that motherfucker. He wasn't ever right for you. You just ran to the first nigga that didn't remind you of me." He laughed.

"I ran because your wife threatened to kill me."

"She wasn't gonna kill you."

"Well, I wasn't gonna stick around and fuckin' find out." I walked over and grabbed my purse and car keys. "I'll be back. I'm going to my house to see what I can find out while he's at work. I know you think it it's not important, but he was here, and if he wanted to, with one phone call he could shut us down."

I left Redd standing there to digest the information I gave him. This shit had to be contained. If Trent so much as blinked in the direction of the police they could have us on prostitution, drug possession with the intent to distribute, not to mention my entire identity was false. I didn't have time to live in Redd's world where everything would be okay. I had to move fast and find out what was really going on.

I jumped into the only possession Trent had left me with and raced to my home. Trent should be at work and it wasn't really like him to come home in the middle of the day. I glanced at the clock on the radio. It was 12:54 pm, that gave me approximately two hours to find some piece of evidence that would fill in the blanks for me. Trent had seemed like everything I desired in a man, but what I desired at the time of arriving in Houston was anything that was different from Redd.

Until twelve years ago, I led my life in the streets. I lived by the streets and always knew I would die in these streets. But when I met Trent all of that changed. I started to believe that I could really be this woman with the perfect life. I believed I could really be Kyra.

After a thirty-minute drive, I pulled up to the house I had until the other day called my home. I sat in the car staring at the massive structure. The French provincial style home was the perfect balance of art and symmetry. I loved this home and being forced out of it was like losing a loved one. I exited the car and headed towards the large wrought iron double doors and entered the keypad entry code. I doubted if Trent changed the code, he always left those things to me and in the past, I had happily obliged if that meant I got to keep playing Kyra.

I could hear the click of my heels hitting the marble floors as I made my way towards his home office. If Trent had any evidence or secrets they would be hidden behind this door. I grasped the cool knob and turned to allow myself entry. An eerie nervousness washed over me. I had every right to be in this home yet I felt as if I was breaking and entering. I was nervous about what Trent would do if he found me in here. He had shown me a side of himself I had never seen before. He was never aggressive or violent with me until now.

I found my way to the plush desk chair and sank into its indulgent comfort. My hand danced around the touch screen to awaken the computer. Blue light illuminated from the screen; the blinking cursor was demanding I put in a code. Code? I had no idea what that could be. I never bothered this computer because I had my own laptop, and until now I completely trusted Trent to be the predictable man I had always known.

Attempting to crack the mystery of how much Trent knew I hurriedly typed in multiple guesses trying to unlock the computer.   With each wrong password the screen shook and made a loud noise as if to say "Bitch try again." I stared blankly at the screen. According to the big bold letters above the password box, I had one attempt remaining before I was completely locked out.

My body fell against the back of the leather chair. This was my last try. What could it be? I rummaged through papers and files hoping to find some clue as to what the password was. I grabbed a black leather planner that I had never seen before. I flipped through the pages. Each page held three columns with different numbers in each one. I had no idea what this was, but I only had one try and there was no way I had time to try all three pages of numbers.

I flipped through the back of a book and saw letters scribbled on a blank page. It had no labels, no other words; it only had the eight characters hurriedly scratched on the page in Trent's handwriting. I slowly typed the letters in knowing this would be my last try. I hit enter on the keyboard and watched the screen go blank before the bright screen light was back. It worked. I tossed the book to the side and scanned his open documents. Trent never closed down any of his browsing or window history.

I browsed the first open window I saw. It was opened to a banking page, but I didn't recognize this bank. I hit the password box and to my surprise login and password information automatically populated. Once I logged in the amount almost blew me away. There was twenty-million dollars in this account.

I clicked to scroll through the transaction history. Money had steadily flowed in and out of this account on a regular. The history was never ending which led me to believe the account had been opened for a while. I clicked on the pdf version of the bank statement. It had my name and address but it was something that I had never seen and I didn't set up.

"Son of a bitch!"

I searched his history and found three accounts in my name. And we aren't talking about a little money, these accounts held millions. All this time I thought I had my secrets and turns out he had far more. I didn't really understand what any of this meant at the moment, but I did know something was way off.

In my old life, I would have never been so stupid. A man would never have complete and utter control over my life. I wanted to have a "normal" life so bad with a man I thought I had control over I had completed neglected to see things for what they really were.

My face burned with anger as I searched for any idea of where this money could be coming from. I looked towards the open closet door and saw a safe. What the hell was in there? I jumped out of the desk chair so forcefully the chair rolled back and collided with the wall. The jarring thud of the chair hitting the wall startled me, but couldn't stop me from getting to that safe. I stared at the black steel box, concentrating on the buttons. What was it with the men and safes?

Redd had a safe but was too stupid to realize he couldn't keep opening it with me there without realizing that I would eventually figure out the code. Now I stood before a safe that I didn't even know Trent had but I would crack it too. I stared at the buttons and noticed that four of the buttons were slightly more worn than the others. The wheels in my head furiously turned. I was going to figure out the code.

I stepped back and eyed the keypad, and then just by chance I decided to try his birthday. It couldn't really be that easy, could it? The most worn keys utilized the same numbers as his birthday. 0-8-1-2, I slowly entered the numbers into the glowing keypad hoping it would accept the code. There were three beeps followed by the sound of something turning, and then it granted me entrance. For such a smart man his ass sure seemed dumb. The password might as well have been password.

I reached in and pulled out the contents of the safe. There was nothing overtly suspicious as a perused the envelopes and papers. I saw his passport, a few credit cards, and some paperwork. My eyes stealthy roamed the contents of the safe, attempting to devour as much information as possible. I wanted to know more about the bank account I had found.

My name was on a lot of the paperwork I found in the safe, there were property deeds, business contracts all listing me as the director. All of these companies I "managed" were all in other countries. I honestly had no idea what I was looking at but whatever it was it wasn't right. How long had this man been using me?

I placed all the papers along the desk, grabbed my phone and quickly started taking pictures of the documents. I would comb through them once I had more time to sit and decipher what all of this really meant.

Peering into the safe it appeared to be empty, but it wasn't exactly eye level so to be sure, I shoved my hand to the back of the black box. I pulled out one last envelope tucked in the back. I undid the clips holding the tanned paper container closed and dumped its contents on the desk as well. A driver's license and passport with my name but Queen's picture spilled out.

"What the hell," I didn't understand what was happening. I scanned the documents; they looked just as authentic as my own. He was planning something, but I had no idea what the hell that was. And what part did Queen actually play in all this? I told Redd countless times that he couldn't trust her. I snapped more pictures before shoving everything back into the safe. I also took down the banking information and password for safekeeping.

I hurriedly placed things back in their original place. Once I was satisfied with the placement of everything I quickly left the house and jumped in my car. I was running out of my own home, but I wanted no chance of running into Trent. After his unusual behavior, I wasn't too sure about his next move. After hearing the clicking sound of my seatbelt being secured, I started the car and hit the gas. I needed to find a place to think, without distraction so I could figure this shit out, fast.

***

*I finally settled into life with Trent and I had to admit things were good. Walking away from that bullshit with Jacob had paid off. He had kept his word to keep my secret and I never had to use what I had on him.*

*I leaned over the pot on the stove and inhaled the rich aroma of the seafood gumbo I was preparing. Even though I had fully become Kyra, there was a little of Dominique that surfaced ever now and again.*

*"Kyra!"*

*"I'm here love." Trent walked into the kitchen and kissed me. Here lately he's seemed a little unlike himself. Trent stood in the kitchen staring at the pot but saying nothing.*

*"Are you okay?"*

*"Yeah, it smells good baby." Trent turned towards our room and then stopped. His gaze caught mine and he looked as if he wanted to say something.*

*"What is it?"*

*"Nothing"*

*"Talk to me." I had truly come to love Trent and when there was something wrong I could definitely tell.*

Trent walked back towards me and pulled me close. His breath was hot against my ear as he whispered. "Let's take a walk." He grabbed my hand and pulled me towards the door. I pulled back to stop him, I needed to turn the pot off.

"Trent, baby we can talk here, I'm cooking." I caressed his face attempting to ease the momentary flickers of panic I saw.

"Let's take that walk. It's been a while since we strolled together." Even though his tone was cool and upbeat, his eyes told a completely different story. He reached for my hand again guided me out of the door. Once we made it towards the entrance of our semi-circular driveway, He finally began to speak.

"There are things about me that I haven't been upfront about. Things that I thought I would never have to say aloud." I looked at Trent, what could he possibly be lying to me about.

"What do you mean?"

"I need to know I can trust you." His words were like a sharp blow. If this man only knew the lengths I went to have his back

"Whatever it is, we'll figure it out." I swallowed trying to clear the lump from my throat. "I know a thing or two about secrets."

*I faced Trent, maybe it was time for us to both stop keeping secrets.*

# CHAPTER 14

Aimlessly I guided my car through the streets of Houston. I didn't want to go back to the house and deal with Redd. He just didn't seem to get it. I felt more alone than I ever had in my life. The support I wanted from Redd was non-existent and what I thought I had found in Trent wasn't there either. I was used to being on my on, but the time I had spent as Kyra had shown me I could have more than what the streets alone could offer.

There was so much information floating around in my head. I found a bank account with my name on it, with millions of dollars in it. I had evidence that Trent was planning something that included Queen, but what?

My first thought was to confront him with proof but I had to figure out what was going on first, figuring out what part Queen played in this was crucial. If I confronted him with no evidence she would know undoubtedly that I knew something and I didn't want to tip off Trent.

I pulled into the Uptown Park shopping center. I loved the Galleria area and I decided that I needed a nice secluded spot where I could think. I parked and headed towards Uptown Sushi, one of my favorite sushi spots. I walked through the door and stood at the hostess counter. The young lady at the desk greeted me with a smile.

"Good afternoon, welcome to Uptown Sushi." I usually had a reservation, but with it being the middle of the day I knew I would be okay. This place got really busy on weekends and evenings, but looking around the beautifully decorated building I knew I would have no trouble with being seated.

"How many?"

"It's just me."

"Okay just a moment, and we will have you seated." She smiled and stepped away. I waited impatiently. I was ready to be seated, have a Lychee martini, seaweed salad, their lickety split roll and devour the information I found in Trent's office.

"Hey!" A sweet and sultry voice invaded my quiet moment. I turned to face the intrusion.

"Hhhhey," The words hesitantly escaped my lips. Michelle smiled; her big brown eyes were deep caverns of innocence. It seemed innocent but I honestly didn't trust it.

The hostess returned, "Will your friend be joining you?"

"Yes, I will," I started to object but decided against making a scene just because we sat at the same table didn't mean I had to talk to her. My plan was to have my lunch and drink in peace. If she chose to tag alone and be ignored, so be it.

She seated us in one of the semi-circular shaped booths along the wall. I slid in towards the middle of the table. Michelle waited for me to be seated comfortably before sliding into the spot right next to me. This booth could honestly fit at least 6 people comfortably, why the hell was she all up on me when there was so much space.

I glanced at Michelle with a raised eyebrow. She didn't seem to notice my unspoken question or maybe she just didn't care. I moved over to give some space between us without making myself uncomfortable and waited for our waitress to take our order.

After ordering I pulled out my phone and started to read over the many documents I had found. Michelle was very silent and I could feel her watching me. Why did she seem to study me so much? Why did she seem to always be around? I placed my iPhone down on the table, now turning all my attention to Michelle. She was openly staring at me, not trying to hide it at all.

"Michelle, how is it do you always seem to be around?"

"What do you mean?"

"I mean you're always around Michelle, lurking in the corner watching, jumping into people's bathtubs, all of that. Why?" I asked the question, never believing that she would honestly answer but it was worth a shot. I am not sure if she wanted Redd, if she thought she was coming for my spot by trying to get close to me or what. It was hard to say. She was never around Redd like this, it was always me she seemed to find those alone moments with.

Maybe they had something going on that I didn't know about and she was trying to make sure that whatever we had was dead. Hell, I don't know what her problem was but I was a little tired of her always seeming to be just coincidently around.

"I'm not lurking." Her head flew back in laughter.

"You're always around or coming around the corner watching me. Now you're here too."

"No, I live there not lurking, and I'm here because I like sushi." She laughed even louder as if I had said something funny. "Maybe I like being around you, you ever consider that?"

"No."

Michelle smiled and closed the gap I had purposely placed between us. "You look like you have a lot on your mind Dominque. You want to talk about something? Tell me what you're really running from."

I decided not to answer. I did have a lot on my mind but I wanted to change the subject from away from me. I picked up my phone and began to read through the documents again.

"What's that?" She asked.

"My business," I placed the phone face down and turned my attention back to Michelle. "So you were in school right, how's that going?" I decided to grill her instead of the other way around. I wanted to see if she could remember what she told me.

She had books and sometimes looked like she was studying but hell I had a lot of things that looked a certain way, so that didn't mean shit. I didn't trust Michelle but since she was always thrusting herself into my space I thought it would be smart to know what and who I'm dealing with.

"It's good, I'm almost done. Was definitely able to pay my tuition off a lot faster than I thought. Thanks to you guys."

"Well, you should thank that one client you have." Michelle just shrugged. My sarcastic tone was lost on her. Most of the girls had regular clients, but Michelle only had one. We didn't argue with it because he paid for her constant availability. He didn't seem like the type but then again I learned a long time ago there wasn't really a type.

He only came once a week, but he paid for her time as if he was seeing her daily. I don't know what she did that was so special to make a man pay for time he wasn't getting. I had even checked the camera to see exactly what his request was, but the only thing I ever caught was him covering the camera.

"I thank him." Michelle tilted her head back and chuckled. My gaze fell on the heart shaped necklace she always wore. I watched as her hands found the gold chain and twirled it around her fingers.

"See something you like?" Her lips curled as her tongue darted around her lips, ending with a slow seductive smile.

"I know things have happened in the past that may have given you the wrong idea, but I like dick."

I needed to make things very clear with her. I wasn't sure what energy I was feeling with her, but I needed her to understand, whatever she thought was happening was not going to happen. Michelle leaned even closer to me as if to challenge my words.

I could smell the sweet scent of her perfume as she inched closer towards me. I felt her hands run the length of my thigh. She pushed my thighs apart and gently pulled my panties to the side. Her touch was delicate and explorative.

"Stop!"

I reached to grab her hand. What the hell did she think she was doing? I pulled away and picked up my phone to go through the information again. I logged into the online account and checked the banking balance again. It's as if I couldn't look at it enough. I had to keep checking to make sure it was still there.

"What are you looking at?"

"You have a problem with minding your business don't you?"

"It looks like banking info, maybe I can help?" I cut my eyes towards her. Damn, she was all in my business. "No, seriously maybe I can help. Business and numbers are my thing, it's what I'm going to school for. You keep looking at your account what are you trying to figure out?"

My instincts told me to shut her down, she seemed like she was always fishing for information. My body fell against the plush backing of the booth as I allowed her words to sink in. Could she really help and what's the risk if I did use her for information? It's not like she knew anything about me.

"I don't need any help." I moved to get up from the table. My finance degree might have been faker than a three dollar bill but I had worked in a bank long enough to know more than a little bit about money. As I reached for my purse Michelle grabbed my hand,

"Maybe you need more help than you know."

I snatched my hand away and headed towards the door, never giving her words another thought.

# CHAPTER 15

Something about Michelle bothered me. I couldn't quite figure her out but I would have to table that for another day. The money was still in the accounts and I hadn't decided what I should do. I knew one thing. I was tired of this victim shit. I felt like I had been abandoned. Abandoned by Trent, a man that I thought genuinely loved me who until Redd showed up I thought I loved back.

Redd and I had our ups and downs but could I trust him. I wonder if we could just disappear in the wind. I pulled into the driveway of the house I used to make money. From the outside it looked like a typical suburban home, no one would ever suspect what really went on behind those walls. I walked through the empty halls searching for Redd.

I needed to feel him out. We hadn't had very much one on one time because I have been so consumed with trying to protect my secrets. But the more I thought about it the more I said to hell with my secrets. Redd was from my past. He knew me and I knew him. It seemed a hell of a lot easier with him than to try to figure shit out with Trent.

It was eerily quiet as I walked into the house. I made my way into the camera room and began to turn all the monitors on. It would be easier to use the cameras to find him rather than walk the whole damn house calling him. I turned my attention to one of the downstairs bedrooms. The camera system had no sound but I could clearly see what was happening.

I watched as Redd lifted Queen unto the bed. His hands greedily caressed her body, touching her the same way he touched me. Their lips met and he hungrily kissed her. She eagerly accepted. My blood boiled as the scene played out. I know that was his wife, but I never had to see it. Back home he kept us pretty separate. I stayed out of her way and for the most part, she stayed out of mine.

"Anything good playing?" Michelle stood in the doorway. Her eyes darted from the screen to my face and back to the screen. "This isn't the first time this happened you know."

"Not the first time for what to happen, Michelle." I breathed through clenched teeth. It was almost as if she was amused. She slinked sexily towards me, never taking her eyes off of me.

"It's not the first time he's fucked his wife here." I watched as a smile spread across her lips. Was she trying to get under my skin? Her words hit me with the force of a tidal wave. Here was thinking of cutting Redd on my newfound ortune, but cutting him in would mean cutting Queen in too.

"I thought he was yo man? Maybe that's what you thought too?" She leaned back against he monitors, twirling her heart locket between ner fingers. The screen began to glitch; it had never done that before. I dismissed the glitch and Michelle's question didn't even deserve an answer. I didn't have time for this bullshit.

The hurried clicks of my five inch heels hitting the wood floors echoed throughout the house as I dashed towards the back of the house where Redd and Queen were. Damn, I really couldn't figure this shit out. Queen seemed to be playing ooth sides, a position I knew all too well.

"What the fuck is she doing here?" Redd ifted his head from between Queen's legs, obviously surprised by my presence. He stared at me while wiping his face with his hands. In this moment I began to wonder what in the hell did I see in him. I had allowed yesterday's feelings to cloud today's judgment when dealing with him. He tilted his head to the side and smirked before he began to speak.

"If I'm here she can be here, who the fuck are you to question me about my wife?" Queen jumped up from the bed, throwing her clothes back on in one swift motion.

"Bitch, I swear I'm so tired of your ass. shoulda got rid of you a long time ago."

Queen started to lunge towards me but was soon stopped by Redd. She always seemed to be stopped by Redd.

"I got this," Redd stretched out his arm to silence Queen before continuing. "Dominque we do what we do and that's it. This is a business arrangement. You owe me money, money that you stole from me. You're fun to fuck," he laughed, "and fuck with. But this, this right here," he pointed towards Queen, " is Wifey, you just my hoe."

Redd's words hit me with the force of a Mack truck. Everything we had been through seemed to flash before my eyes. I know this started as a business arrangement but years and years of him laying in my bed said it wasn't. The only reason I left with that money was because of his wife. I deserved that shit. Who did this nigga really think he was talking too?

"Your hoe nigga? That's not what your ass be saying and claiming when you inside of me. Fuck you and your wifey, you know she's fucking my husband right."

Queen moved Redd's hand to the side and moved towards me. Her hair was disheveled from her brief sex session I interrupted. Her eyes were ablaze as she walked. This bitch looked like a woman who was quickly becoming unhinged. Queen stood so close to me I could smell the scent of Redd's dick on her breath. She leaned in and whispered so that only I could hear.

"I'm not only gonna fuck your husband, remember what I said bitch, I'm gonna fuck your life. Nice and slow. I'm gonna tear this shit up."

"I am so done with this shiiiiiiiiiiiit!" I shoved Queen's small frame against the wall and away from me. Before she could react I was on Redd. I scanned the room for the nearest object that could do the most damage. My eyes quickly fell on the bedside lamp, not even bothering to unplug it I grabbed it and hurled it towards Redd's head. They have me fucked all the way up if they think I'm just going to sit here and deal with their shit. I grabbed my keys and bag and headed for my car.

"I'm gonna kill that bitch Redd."

"Fuck her, she ain't never been shit but a side bitch with main chick ambitions. Our plan solid, we don't need the bitch no more." I didn't know what plan he was talking about and I didn't slow down to find out.

"Where are you going?" Michelle followed closely behind, jumping in my car as I unlocked the door.

"Michelle, I don't have time for this bullshit,

get the hell out of my car." I don't know wha
games she was playing, or why she thought i
was cool to jump in my car like we besties, we
ain't shit. Half the time I can't figure out he
angle.

"You seem like you need someone on you
team, let me be that for you. You held me down
gave me somewhere to stay, help me make
money, let me help you now."

I didn't know how she planned on helping
me, but right now it didn't matter. I quickly
weighed my options, was Michelle friend or foe
After a moment of pondering, something told
me it was better to have her as an ally.

"Fine, close the door," I shouted as I hit the
gas pedal and sped off.

# CHAPTER 16

The ocean breeze swept across my skin as I stood on the balcony of our Galveston hotel suite. The morning air felt good against my exposed skin as I scrolled through my phone. We had been here for a week compliments of Michelle's client's credit card. I knew my time was winding up and I would need to come up with something fast.

I checked the accounts daily, I knew I was going to make a play for the money but when I did it I needed to be prepared to disappear. I had no discussions with Trent since he threw me flat out on my ass.

"Coffee?" I reached out to take the warm cup of coffee and resumed my gaze into the ocean.

"Still don't trust me huh."

"I trust no one."

"I told you I just wanna help."

"You don't even know me to wanna help me. So what is it that you want?"

Michelle didn't bother to answer my

question. She sat next to me, too close as usual and wrapped her arms around me. My body tensed as she pulled me close to her.

"You look like you need a hug."

"I'm not gay Michelle."

"Neither am I." She whispered, pulling me into her. I released a sigh. I was too tired to fight. It felt nice to lean on someone even if I didn't trust that someone. I realized I've had a long history of using sex and people to escape what I was going through, but at this moment I really didn't give a damn. Escape was the magic word and I might as well use her.

She nibbled my neck, moving upward until her lips found mine. She began to kiss me. It was sweet at first, then with each passing second, it filled me with overwhelming desire. I welcomed the distraction. I needed to feel something other than the panic I felt inside that increased with each passing moment.

Her hands explored my body. I had never been this intimate with a woman in a one on one situation but she had me intrigued. I could hear the sound of the Gulf gently rising and falling against the beach as she planted tiny kisses against my body.

The warmth of her touch was welcomed. Softer than Trent's or Redd's ever was, yet just as strong. She pulled my maxi dress above my head, exposing my naked body on the balcony. I briefly wondered if anyone else could see, but the thought of someone watching me turned me on even more.

Michelle nestled her head between my legs. Her tongue pushed forward and parted my lips. She ran tiny circles around my clitoris. This shit felt amazing. Her head pushed further and further into my wetness. She wasn't scared of getting her face a wet, I think she was trying to drown in it and I didn't mind.

My nipples hardened as her tongue eagerly circled my clitoris. I watched as her fire red nails traveled up my thighs, landing on my breast. My reddish brown peaks stood at full attention as she squeezed, intensifying my pleasure. I could feel her fingers slide inside my wetness, her come-hither motion causing her finger to tap against my g-spot.

"I'm gonna make that pussy cum for me!" Damn, she sounded so sexy. She stood above me and slipped her clothes off all in one motion. I admired her body. From where I was sitting it seemed perfect. She stood motionless, never moving her eyes off of me. She peered so deeply into me I had to look away.

I diverted my gaze and allowed my eyes to fall on her full round breast. I wanted to touch her. I didn't know what her next move would be but my body shivered with anticipation. She pushed me against patio lounge chair. Her body moved cautiously towards me, gently pushing my legs apart as she got closer. Her chestnut colored eyes locked with mine as our bodies grazed against one another. The heat from her body further ignited my passion.

Placing my legs on her shoulders Michelle's soft body collided with mine. I felt her full lips connect to mine. Her tongue parted my lips and I could taste my sweetness on her. I wrapped my arms around her and pulled her even closer to me. I couldn't get enough of the feeling she was giving me. Her thumb moved back and forth against my clit.

"Damn that feels so good."

"I want that pussy to cum for me. Cum for me baby." Michelle's fingers slide inside of me two at a time. She thrust inside of me tapping that damn spot and rubbing my clit over and over again. My moans became louder. This shit had my body on fire with desire.

Her touch was feminine but strong, like the culmination of both masculine and feminine energy. My body craved as much of her as possible. I arched my back and threw my head back. This was so close to ecstasy. The evidence of my excitement rolled down my thighs.

" I bet you no man has ever fucked you this

good. Squirt for me baby." Our bodies crashed as I started to raise my hips higher, desperate for more. I ran my hands through her hair cupping the back of her head, pulling her towards me, my actions demanding that she kiss me.

My tongue was eager to meet hers as my hips moved faster, and she pushed her fingers as far as they could go. I tightened my legs around her shoulders. I could literally feel every muscle in my body tighten. The pressure was building inside and I was about to burst.

"Oh my gooooooooooooood!" I shouted as a wave of pleasure washed over me. A steady current of wetness flowed before my body went completely limp. I could barely catch my breath.

Michelle's body fell against mine with her head resting against my stomach. We spoke no words, but my mind moved nonstop to make sense of what just happened.

"Tell me one thing about you Dominque." She broke the silence.

"There's nothing to tell."

"I think there is, tell me about your husband. What does he do? How did you guys get here? I know you're not going home anymore at night."

"Sometimes you really don't know who people really are. You know." A solemn feeling washed over me and we were silent again.

"Hey, I'm going to take a shower." I wanted to end this uncomfortable silence and I didn't want Michelle getting the wrong idea about what had happened. I had heard all the jokes about lesbians and uhuals and I didn't need her thinking we were about to be moving in together. Michelle sat up allowing me to get up. I could feel her eyes ravaging my body as I walked towards the bathroom.

# CHAPTER 17

I stood in front of the mirror trying to get my head in the game. Whatever that was between Michelle and me was nothing more than a distraction. I slipped into a pair of skinny jeans and a tank top not even bothering to put on a bra.

I reached for the complimentary lotion and began to rub it onto my exposed areas. I glanced down and noticed Michelle's necklace lying on the counter. I picked it up. I don't know why I cared but it must have meant something to her because I never saw her with it off.

"Hey Michelle, you left your necklace in here." I exited the steamy bathroom and walked toward the sitting area. Michelle was still outside. She stood with her back turned to the large wall length balcony door.

I moved closer so she could hear me. She turned around holding my phone.

"What are you doing with my phone?" I left it on the balcony. I was so distracted by what happened between Michelle and me, I had forgotten all about it.

"Nothing. I was about to bring it in." I eyed her suspiciously. I reached and grabbed my phone before turning to go back in the room. I didn't want her eyes on any of the documents had found in the house. I sat at the foot of the bed and looked towards Michelle. Her eyes probed, I assumed to gauge my reaction.

"You're so beautiful. I can't believe your husband and Redd let you get away." Her statement seemed more like a question. She had hinted so many times she wanted to know more about me. But until I could figure out her angle I wasn't going to tell her shit.

"Here, you left this in the bathroom." I held my hand out, handing her the gold trinket she always wore. Her hand grazed against mine as she reached for it. A jolt of electricity surged through me. What was happening? Her presence was making me uncomfortable.

"Maybe I can give you my heart." Michelle leaned over and clamped her necklace around my neck.

"Michelle...I..."

"Don't worry about it, I don't expect yours. Yet. " She leaned in and kissed me. Her lips were like plush pillows. I closed my eyes and exhaled. It felt good to be desired. Was I that desperate for affection that I was willing to go against everything in me that screamed stop?

"I have to go."

"Don't forget the keycard. I'll be here waiting for you for round two."

I swiftly swiped my keys off of the dresser they sat on and rushed away from the room. I do not have time for this shit. I needed to think and get my ass out of the hole it was in. Trent flipped on me, Redd flipped on me and now Michelle, who I didn't even know was trying to give me her heart.

Sliding into the plush leather seat of the only possession I had been left with, I started the ignition and peeled off. I needed this moment of solitude to think. The same thought had been playing over and over in my head. Take the money, Dominque and that's just what I planned to do. I think my time as Kyra had run its course, it's time to leave my past and my present behind and create a future. To do that I would need to go back to where I started.

After an hour in this ridiculous Houston traffic, I landed right back where I started. Not much had changed in this neighborhood, and I was hoping that Berto could still be found.

I pulled in front the familiar small two-bedroom house. Everything still looked the same. The yard was not manicured. There were bars on the window and there was always people on the porch. To an untrained eye there were hanging out, but to someone like me, someone who had seen these streets before, I knew those dudes were not to be fucked with. They were your way in and your way out.

I pushed the driver's side visor down to check my appearance. I pushed my hair away from my face and put on my shades. I eyed the necklace Michelle had given me.

"No," I said as I released the pendant from my neck. I dropped it into the cup holder between the two front seats and exited the car.

"Hey, Berto here?"

"Who's askin'?"

"Dominique" The guys on the steps eyed me suspiciously. One of the men step to the side and began to mumble inaudibly into his cell phone.

"Alright, c'mon." I followed the man inside but was stopped immediately after the door closed. My heart raced. It hadn't been this hard to see Berto the first time around, but something told me that just maybe this was a whole different operation. The man waived one of those wand style metal detectors over me and then patted me down.

"Open your shirt."

"What? Open my shirt? I'm not taking my fucking clothes off." I was confused by his equest.

"You will if you want to see him." I undid the buttons of my shirt. Obviously now satisfied, the man stepped to the side. "She's clean. Follow me."

I followed him through the house. It was extremely cold inside. This might have been the same house on the outside, but it was totally different on the inside. There were large screens and computers everywhere. Some of them simply flashing random things I didn't understand, others with people working diligently as if they were in an office.

We finally reached the back room I had initially met Berto in. My eyes swept the room. This room looked closer to what I remember. There were cameras backgrounds and printers set up. But this equipment seemed a lot more expensive than the ones I had seen before.

"Thanks, Juan. That will be it for now." Damn, he had stepped his shit up. He had a crew, a for real crew.

"Hi."

"What's up mami, what brings you in?"

"I need some work done for me."

"Kyra not working out for you?" How in the hell had he remembered that, it's been years?

"Sit down." He pointed towards the empty chair in front of his desk.

"It's time to get out of Houston. And I need a little help with moving some money. Maybe you know someone?"

"I got you Ma, what kinda money you wan moved."

"It's a lot, and I want it hidden, completely unable to be traced." I felt like I was asking for a lot. I didn't know anything about this side of things. I worked at a bank and faked my way through a lot of that shit. It was only a way to make my fake identity seem more legit.

Apart of me was a little scared to hand access to twenty-million dollars, but I had a plan and this was apart of it. We had done business before and he had given me exactly what I paid for. I pulled my phone out of my purse and typed in the username and password I had stolen from Trent's office.

"This is what we are talking about." I placed the phone in front of him, not even wanting to say the amount out loud.

"Damn, " Berto said while sitting back in his chair.

"Can you do it, can you move it into another account? But so that it can't easily be traced. Is that possible?" I thought that it was, I had seen shit like this on television, but when it came to real life who knows.

"I got you, but it's gonna cost you. For the new identity and to bounce that much money around it's gonna run you thirty percent of what's in that account. You having the passwords will make it a bit easier but there is still a shit load of risk, so I gotta make it worth my while. And that's me being generous because you know, you're a repeat customer."

He laughed and winked at me. My mind quickly did the math. The last time I checked there was about twenty-five million in that account. That meant that this would cost more than seven million dollars. I knew it wouldn't be cheap but after this, I didn't want to be found. This was way more money than I had stolen from Redd, and I knew with this I could be set. What was seven million compared to seventeen million, nothing? I shrugged my shoulders and extended my hand.

"It's a deal. When will it be ready?"

"Come back in a few days."

"One more thing Berto, I need another car."

"Yea, see my cousin." He typed an address into my phone.

Before leaving I left Berto the information he would need for the account. Then he walked me to the door and called the guy who had let me in to see me out. I glanced again at the computers and the people working on them. A smile spread across my face. For the first time in months, I felt excited about something. I was so close to being away from this bullshit I could almost feel the Miami breeze against my skin.

# CHAPTER 18

could hear the screeching of my tires against the cement as I swung into the driveway of the house I had gotten for Redd. This was supposed o be my way out, but my debt seemed like a distant memory. I was so eager to keep my life ogether and had somehow destroyed.

I hurriedly exited the car and headed into he house. I was out of money, had no access to my accounts with Trent so I decided to do what I do best, take that shit. Redd obviously had played me. He used me to make his money like he always had. For him, I had always been good business. So I considered this getting back what was mine. I needed just enough to hold me until Berto got my stuff together.

I eased the door open slowly. I didn't believe that Redd was here but you could never know. I moved as fast as my legs could take me. I wanted to avoid running into him. After I had come in and watched him with that bitch he called a wife, I knew it wouldn't be pleasant between the two of us.

A disgusting smell hit me as I moved through the house. None of the bitches had bothered to clean. This shit had gone from high class to trash in a matter of days. It was filthy and disgusting. walked pass the mess and moved towards the back area with the security monitors and money As soon as I entered the room I grabbed the metal box he kept the money in. Every night he was supposed to dump the mini safe so there was never much money here. This was one time I hoped that Redd didn't listen to me.

I grabbed the cold plastic handled and opened it. The black metal box was practically empty. I grabbed the cash that was inside Sometimes we charged the customers through a fake company but the PayPal card wasn' here. I counted the cash that was here, less than a thousand dollars. What the hell had he been doing? I stuffed the bills into my purse, returned the box to its original position and left the room.

The house was dead silent. I walked towards the front room and took in my surroundings one more time. Redd had played me, and I had allowed it.I was never supposed to be caught up in this bullshit. I was only supposed to be here long enough to pay him his money back and had done that and more.

My skin became heated and anger washed over me. Standing in this room made me feel nothing but uneasiness and chaos. I had given this man more than his money back, I had given him a resource to constantly make money and his dumb ass couldn't even see the potential. Redd could kiss my ass. I be damned if he would prosper off of me after I was gone.

I thought he was that person I could always keep it one hundred with, but it was the same shit different day. When it came down to it, when he looked at me he saw dollar signs. Nothing more. I heard him tell Queen their plan was solid, and if their plan was to prosper off of what I had built then they were gonna need to think again.

I ran to the garage looking for whatever I could find to do the most damage. I could tear up this whole place, take out the monitors, destroy the beds, but I knew that wouldn't bother Redd, he didn't give a shit about those monitors, that was my idea, and he didn't give a damn about those beds, he'd just tell them to fuck on the floor.

There wasn't really anything in the garage. I turned to leave but not before slamming my foot into a can. I looked down and noticed a small gas can. I don't even know when this got here because Redd didn't take care of the place, maybe the lawn man left it, but who really cares.

I picked up the small container and began to shake. I practically wanted to do a happy dance when I discovered there was something inside. Instantly I knew what I was about to do. I was going to burn this motherfucker down. If they wanted a plan they can plan to do this shit all over by themselves.

I removed the tiny red cap from the nozzle and began to pour it all over the house. I shook the can to cover the plush carpeting through the lower levels and on the staircase. I rattled the hell out of it until there was nothing left. The scent of gasoline wafted through the air, making me sick to my stomach. It was time to get this over with. I went to the kitchen to grab a lighter. It felt good to purge my pass. I can't believe I wasted so much time on Redd.

My hand slightly shook as I clicked the lighter normally reserved for candles. I knew I needed to move fast because with the way I tossed around the fuel it was going to catch fast. I steadied my hand and slowly moved it towards the seat nearest the door. My left hand gripped the handles of my purse. Damn, I should have opened the door.

The flamed made contact with the chair. Tiny flames began to dance across the doused fabric, growing larger as they began to connect. The heat from the mounting fire jolted me into action. I needed to get out of here.

Still clutching the lighter, I ran out of the door and jumped in my car, backed out and was gone. My lips spread into a satisfied smirk, I was finally taking back control.

# CHAPTER 19

My left hand clutched the steering wheel as I dug to find my cell phone at the bottom of my purse. It was time to get rid of this car. And it's about time I started acting like myself. Dominque was too smart for the bullshit. Finally finding my cell phone, I dialed the number Berto had given me earlier. The phone rang forever before someone finally answered.

"What."

"Hey, I wanna know if I can come by. I need something new."

"Who gave you this number?"

"Berto."

"Come in an hour. I'll be here." The rude man said, then abruptly disconnected the call. I didn't care if he hung up the phone or not. I needed another car, to get out of this got damn city.

I glanced at the clock on my dash. It was 7:37 pm. I could be there by nine and get this over with. Then head back to the hotel and fight Michelle off until I was outta here.

My cell phone began to ring. I needed to make a mental note to get a new one of those too. I couldn't have people being able to find me once I was gone.

"What the fuck did you do?"

"What the fuck does it look like asshole?' This dumb ass didn't deserve my time. My thumb found the small red circle and I disconnected the call. I was done with that bullshit. As soon as I tossed it into the seat it began to ring again I clicked the button on the side placing it in vibrate mode and continued to steer my car towards my next destination.

The lights from the car behind me were glaringly bright. The driver began to flash his high beams on and off. What the hell was he doing? I maneuvered the car into the next lane to allow the car to pass. As soon as I moved over he moved over. It was starting to get dark and I didn't know what kind of game this person was playing. You never know with this city, road rage could come out of nowhere.

I hit the gas and started to haul ass. Because I was unfamiliar with the neighborhood, I wanted to get out of this area as fast as I could. The faster I moved the faster they followed. I jumped on the freeway. I felt like I had better chances of getting away from this pyscho if I could disappear down the highway. My GPS kept telling me to make the next legal U-turn, but right now I wanted to get away from the person following me.

I tried to calm down. It could have been some random guy that liked what they saw. It's happened to me before. But the vehicle behind me continued to follow me a little too long, maybe he was just eager. I checked the rearview again. I didn't see the car. I exhaled a sigh of relief maybe they were gone.

I hit my signal to exit the freeway and turn around. I needed to get this car situation done. I looked over my shoulder to check my blindside moments before the vehicles collided. The screeching sound of metal hitting metal jarred me. My entire body tensed as my car began to spiral down the exit ramp. From wall to wall the car bounced before coming to a complete stop.

Before I could check and see if anything was broken. The black SUV that had been following me pulled up behind me. A man jumped out the passenger side and headed towards my car.

"Noooo, Noooo!" I screamed. I could only see his eyes peering into my window. His face was completely covered but he looked menacing. The man yanked the door open and grabbed me by my hair.

"Get the fuck out bitch!" His commanded. I was completely frozen. What in the hell was happening? I couldn't understand why this was happening. He dragged me by my hair until he had successfully removed me out of the car. Everything moved so fast. My eyes darted from left to right attempting to make eye contact with anyone that would help me. There was no one.

"Move." The man shoved some hard object into my back. He pushed me until I reached the black Escalade.

"No, I'm not getting in there." I didn't know what waited for me inside of the SUV. I pushed back against the man as hard as I could. "Let me go!" The man fell against the safety rail. This was my chance. I began to run, if I could just make it back to my car, dented or not I could maybe make it out of here. I ran around the back of the truck, trying desperately to get back to mine. Thinking I had outsmarted the man, I dashed towards my car which only seemed feet away. I could taste my freedom.

"Where the hell you think you're going?" It was a different voice.

"Agggghhhhhh!" A sharp shooting pain erupted in the back of my head. My hand flew to the spot of the injury as if cradling it would make the pain any less. I blinked my eyes everything was becoming blurry. I shuffled forward, still trying to get away. The more I moved the dizzier I felt. I thought I was moving forward, but I seemed to only moving in circles. I looked up at the streetlight above me.

The bright light glowed, then with each passing second, I saw less and less of the bright light. I could feel the force of gravity pull me to the ground, then everything faded from blurry to black.

# CHAPTER 20

My eyes flew open. I jolted straight up and attempted to take in my surroundings. I don't know how long I had been in the back of this car or even where I was. My hands were tied behind me and my legs were bound together. I struggled to gain my balance and sit up. I was still disoriented from whatever had knocked me out earlier. The stale air inside the car made it difficult for me to breathe.

There was only one man in the front seat of the car. I scanned my surroundings. I had no idea where I was but this area was dark. There was a massive industrial building in front of me. It looked like it hadn't been used in years. It was secluded, and there didn't appear to be any other buildings or business within miles. It was the perfect place to make someone disappear.

We were parked in front. I glanced to my left and I saw my car had been driven here as well. Guess whoever these assholes worked for wanted to leave no evidence. My heart raced because I had no idea what to expect. All I knew is that I wanted out.

"Let me out of this fucking car."

"Shut up."

The man driving turned around and extended his arm. I could see straight down the barrel of the gun. Tiny beads of sweat began to form in every crevice of my body. I fell back against the seat. Who could be doing this to me? Had Berto already moved the money? He told me a few days and it had only been one. Had somebody found out about the money already? Redd didn't have the fucking organizational skills to pull this off and Trent and I hadn't spoken since he threw my ass out. So who would and could kidnap my ass.

"Get out." I didn't argue this time. The gun in his hand was all the incentive I needed to comply. My feet were tied, which made movement extremely difficult. I shuffled behind the man who led me inside the abandoned building.

"Sit down and shut up."

The man in black shoved me towards the ground. More pain shot through my body as I hit the ground. The room was dim, the only light that entered the room escaped from the open door of another room. I pushed myself back against the wall and allowed my head to hit the wall. I winced from the pain. The room was so quiet I could hear the thump of my heart race inside of my chest. I didn't know how I was going to get out of this shit. Light slipped into the room as the door creaked open.

"Get the fuck off of me!"

I watched as they hurled his body in first then hers. They crashed into the ground, landing one on top of the other before being able to gain their balance and sit up. I eyed them. Her hair was disheveled. If they had handled her the same as me, I'm quite certain my appearance was probably very close to hers.

I averted my gaze towards him. He sat on the ground, bound and tied just like us. I watched his chest rise and fall with each angry breath he took. He finally made eye contact.

"What did you do you crazy bitch?"

"I didn't do shit."

"No, you always do something, scheming ass bitch! I'm only in this fuckin city because you stole from me. Then you burn down my means of making money, now I'm being fucking abducted. Yo, bitch you are a fuckin' curse and whatever this shit is, I'm certain you got something to do with it."

Queen was silent as Redd and I went back and forth. She was slumped over, crying while she leaned against Redd. My lips curled into a disgusted snarl. All the shit this bitch did and she's crying.

"Bitch, stop crying. You bad enough to step to me, to try to have me killed now you crying. Bitch please. We don't have time for this shit. We need to figure out why someone would kidnap us."

"I don't know." His voice was full of annoyance.

"You never know shit Redd."

The door flew open; making a loud thud that demanded our attention. We abandoned our conversation. The quiet left an eerie feel in the room. Try abductors entered the room. I pushed myself as far as I could against the wall, trying to disappear. The guard saw me move back and lunged towards me, grabbing me again by my hair.

He began to drag me by my curly locks into the middle of the floor. My kicks were useless against this man's strength. He tossed my body to the ground like I was a hopeless doll he was done playing with.

"Sit here and shut up." I watched as he did the same for Queen and Redd. We were in a straight line in the center of the room. Red was to the left of me and to the left of him was Queen. I couldn't control my heartbeat. I was more than certain now maybe Trent had found out about me taking that money. I planned to be in the wind before anyone knew anything about that, now I was almost certain I wouldn't make it out of this room.

Two more men walked through the door. The light illuminated behind the first man's head. He appeared to be a tall menacing shadow. The second guy followed with the same shadowy mystery as the first. I squinted to make out their faces. As they moved closer the men slowly came into focus. The kidnappers parted to allow them to pass.

They stood shoulder to shoulder, one of them holding an iPad in hand. Looking at them both you could clearly see who was in charge.

"Now," his eyes shifted from left to right. "Which one of y'all took my motherfuckin' money?" Trent's intimidating voice boomed throughout the room. Every ounce of air was sucked out of me when he spoke. I struggled to breathe. Jacob was with him. I knew what it meant, the last time I saw Jacob with somebody they didn't make it out alive.

"Let me, Trent let me, I can…" Queen shook uncontrollably. She was scared. She was only a shell of the person that I remembered. She always had somebody in her corner to fight for her. Now there was no one. Redd couldn't do shit for her right now.

"You can what?" He stepped towards her with his hand cupped around his ear as if he was rying to hear her. "Pick her ass up."

One of the guys in black grabbed her and in one quick move she was standing on her bound eet in front of Trent and Jacob. Her body shook as tears streamed down her cheeks. I couldn't even lie, I was terrified too, but I refuse to give hem the satisfaction of knowing how scared I was.

"So what is it that you want to explain?"

Queen didn't speak. Not one word, she was dead ass quiet. She stood there shaking, attempting to make sounds come out of her open mouth. Her words were incoherent. They sounded like the ramblings of a crazy person.

She turned to look at me. I know this bitch wasn't trying to put her shit off on me. Whatever happened she knew something about, but she was looking at me like I knew what it was. Did this have something to do with their solid plan?

"Why you looking at me?"

"Oh, she working with you? Kyra? But that's not your real name is it?" He directed the last part to me.

"Bullshit, I don't know shit about shit." I made eye contact with the man I've shared a bed with for twelve years. Until now this man had treated me like his queen, now I felt like nothing more than a stranger. My eyes pleaded with him to recognize how sorry I was for bringing all of this into our lives because I thought it would save me, I thought it would save us. He held our locked gaze for a moment and then shook his head like he was trying to dislodge something from his mind.

"Jacob, says that somebody has been dipping into my money. Slowly taking shit that don't belong to them. And I know y'all have something to do with it. And I'm sure this nigga right here" he pointed towards Redd, "put y'all both up to this shit." Trent was pissed. His face was contorted with anger, his eyes ablaze with loathing. I was slowly realizing this is not about the money I was trying to take.

This was about whatever Redd and Queen had been up to. I'm sure Redd was behind this somehow. He thought we were rich and he wanted his share of it. Even if I did give him a way to make his money back, he still wanted more.

Jacob stood silently to the side. He didn't react to any of what was going on and I wasn't surprised. I knew he wasn't what he said he was. He was an attorney but I knew a long time ago he was much more than that. This attorney shit just made it easier to hide, move and protect his money.

"Man, cool it with this bullshit. Don't nobody know shit about what you talking about. You lucky these fake ass niggas got me tied down, otherwise, I would be kicking your ass."

"Then get up and kick my ass then!" Trent walked over and kicked the shit out of Redd. "Motherfucker, you think you can whip my ass? Do you know who the fuck I am?" Trent balled up his fist and hit Redd so hard he fell backward. I had never seen Trent act like this. He had always been so quiet, but the man that stood before me was assertive. He was bossin' up on Redd, and I wasn't sure Redd had what it would take to handle Trent.

"Bitch made motherfucka, it ain't shit to hit a man that's tied up."

"Let him loose," Trent demanded and the men went to work. Redd ran towards Trent, but before Redd could land a punch, Trent was hitting him. Striking him, blow after blow. Blood spewed from his open wounds. He stumbled falling back. He wasn't shit without a gun strapped to him. Without that steel courage of his, he was nothing.

"Stop it! It was me! I transferred the money, I didn't think you would find out. It was so much money in that account. How could you notice a few thousands?" Queen was speaking up to save Redd. She swung her head towards me. "This is all your wife's fault. It's because of her, she ruined our lives. She took our money and built a life with you, and we had nothing. I just wanted her to feel the same."

Trent walked towards Queen. "So you thought you could play me? All that pushing up on me and fluttering your eyelashes my way was so you could steal from me? " Trent bent down eye level with her and spoke through clenched teeth "You're going to put my money back. You took from me, now I'm gonna take from you." He nodded towards Jacob and he proceeded to work the same magic I had seen him work in that underground garage. Queen rattled of answers to Jacobs questions. Within moments it was done.

"It's done." Jacob had watched all of this without so much as blinking. This was just another day to him.

"Give me your gun." Trent stretched his hand out to one of the men. I watched in horror as he gripped the handle of the gun. The loud echo of Trent loading the chamber filled the abandoned warehouse. My body was numb as I watched Trent take slow deliberate steps towards Redd, who was struggling to regain his composure. He stumbled to his feet and tried to hit Trent. Trent raised his hand with lightning speed and then the pop of the bullets flying through the air stopped Redd in his tracks.

"Noooooooo!" Queen screamed as Redd's lifeless body fell to the ground. Blood oozed from the open wound in the middle of his forehead. His eyes were void, staring into nothingness. There was no coming back from that. Queen wailed, her bound hands clawing on the ground, as she struggled to move towards Redd's corpse.

I wanted to say something but no words would come out. My body shook uncontrollably. What the fuck was happening? Trent nodded towards the men then made his exit from the room. He stopped mid-step, just before walking out the door and turned towards me. Our eyes locked only for a moment, then he was gone.

As if that was their cue, the henchmen approached us and slammed the butt of the gun into our skulls. I watched Queen go out like a light. My head throbbed with pain, but I knew on the inside I was a survivor and I was going to make it out of this alive. If I could hold on to my consciousness then maybe I could make it out of this room alive. With everything in me, I fought against the dizzy feeling.

"Why?" I looked up at the man. I struggled to form my sentences, "Please just let us go. Jacob, help me, help –," The crashing sound of the doors tumbling open stunned me. I turned towards the sound of the noise.

"FBI!" Swarms of armed officers rushed into the room, guns drawn. Everyone in the room scattered. I struggled to stand to get out of the way of the men rushing the room.

"Dominique! Dominique! You alright?"

Michelle rushed towards me. Her arms wrapped around me and pulled me to my feet. Her hands were all over me touching me checking me confusing the hell out of me. I stared at her but she seemed different from the woman I had spent the past few months around. Her hair was pulled back into a neat ponytail, she actually had on clothes and vest and badge that read FBI.

"Michelle? What the fuck?"

# CHAPTER 21

don't think she knows much."

"Agent Viera, she has a rap sheet longer than my nine inch cock. She's into everything from prostitution to fraud. What about this woman makes you think she's innocent of anything."

Their hushed voices floated throught the cracked door. This was not apart of my plan. I was supposed to be gone not here. I sat in the sterile gray interrogation room listening to them discuss me. My hands and feet were released from the makeshift shackles that Trent had me bound in and had been replaced with the cold steel of handcuffs. A buzzing sound floated through the room and then she was standing in front of me. None of this made any sense.

"Michelle, what the fuck is going on?"

"I'm S.A. Amina Viera." I stared at her in shock. My mind raced to connect the dots. That's why she was always around. That's why she always wanted to know things. She's been playing me all along, trying to get information out of me.

She sat down in front of me and began to

layout pictures in front of me. "Tell me what you know about the TCC?"

"The what?"

"Third Coast Cartel, don't play dumb, we know you know." The man spoke up.

"Let me handle this Jones," She waved him off and then moved towards me. Whenever she was around she eyed me like I was her prey and now I know why, I was. I held my head down not wanting to make eye contact with her. She lowered her head, forcing me to look at her. Her eyes begged me to answer her. "Dominique this is not looking good for you. Tell us what you know."

"I don't know what you're talking about Michelle, or whoever the fuck you are."

"Tell us what this means." Michelle hit playback on a tablet device and I heard my voice. I was on a phone call, trying setup things to get the hell out of Houston but I wasn't going to tell her that.

"How did you get that?" My mind was moving at lightning speed trying to put things together. I understood but I didn't understand. How did I end up in a damn interrogation room being accused of anything?

"The locket I gave you." She looked at me almost apologetically.

"So you're telling me, you fucked me, gave me some bullshit ass speech about giving me your heart, and then put a listening device on me? And how did you know where to find me?"

"I put a tracking app on your phone. Listen Dominique, you were our way in. We already know your husband is the head of the TCC organization. We also know that the paper trail leads back to you. What was Redd and Queen's role in the organization? What was yours? Talk to us and make it easier on yourself."

Her sneaky ass was out there messing with my phone that day. I had to admit this chick was slick. When she went undercover I guess she went deep. Michelle moved in closer to me, her eyes continually pleading to make contact. Did she really think that shit was going to work?

"I'm not telling you shit. You tell them about all the times you sucked my pussy bitch. You were undercover alright. How did any of that shit help further your case because I never had shit to tell you?" How dare this bitch tell me she bugged me and followed me and she wants me to give her information?

The agent in the corner laughed as he watched our exchange. Every instinct in me told me not to trust her. All that running into her everywhere. Every bit it was an orchestrated dance to try to get me to spill whatever it was she thought I knew. Anger swelled within me, there was no way I was going down like this. I knew nothing about the Third Coast Cartel.

"Give us a minute Jones." Jones questioned the command but quickly exited the room. Michelle got up and moved towards the camera in the room, hit a button on the remote. She pulled a chair close to me, too close as usual and reached and touched my handcuffed hand.

"It wasn't all just me undercover. I felt something."

"Bullshit. You were trying to use me, but I can't help you. I don't know what you're talking about."

"You know more than you're saying. Every questionable account is in your name, property, and everything."

I glanced at the pictures she laid out on the table. A lot of them were lawyers in Trent's firm. I shook my head and sat there in silence. I had no idea how I was going to get out of this. Michelle said she had felt something, could I use that. Probably not, she was obviously an undercover agent. She faked feelings for a living.

Michelle stood and walked back to her file. Her demeanor had changed, and she was all business. She flipped through the pages. I could see one of my mug shots on top. She read in silence for what seemed like forever before she began to speak again.

"I've been on this case for two years. Your husband runs a tight ship. You were my way in. Now help me and I'll help you Dominique. You're facing a lot of charges, prostitution, drug distribution, embezzlement. The list goes on and on so you better start remembering something fast. Or make no mistake I will lock your ass up faster than you spread your legs. I've been working too long on this case and somebody is going down for this shit."

Her words swirled around in my head. I could tell by her tone that she wasn't playing. She felt something but not enough to save my ass from going to jail. I couldn't go to jail, not when I had over 17 million dollars waiting for me in an account somewhere. This wasn't apart of the plan at all.

"Hellooooo, are you listening? Your husband Trent Jamison, is believed to be the leader of the largest drug distribution rings from here to Miami. No one gets close to him. No one new gets in, but somehow you did."

More and more words spilled out of her mouth but I couldn't stop thinking about how I could get out of this. Think Dominique. Damn, I prided myself on knowing how to get out of a situation but how in the hell could I make that happen being handcuffed to this table. These people thought I knew something. I didn't know shit.

"Queen Richardson is in a coma. Lawrence "Redd" Richardson, went in that building and didn't make it back out. Now, why were you there? How were all of you involved?"

She was hitting me with repeated verbal blows. Redd was dead and Queen was in a coma. I sank back into my seat and let the information sink in. I was the only witness, besides Jacob and the men and since they were the ones holding the guns I doubt they would say anything. This means my version of the story was the only version of the story.

"Get me my phone. I'll talk but I need a deal. I want immunity."

"For immunity your info gotta be good Dominique."

"Just do it." I could finally see the light at the end of the tunnel.

# CHAPTER 22

The light peeked into the dim room as I eyed the blue sedan parked outside. For the past three days there was always a car parked outside. I turned to face Michelle.

"How long will I have to stay in this damn house?"

"For however long you have to be here. Now sit down."

"Bossy bitch." I took a seat and eyed her. As she leaned forward to pull something out of her bag her hair fell across her face. I could see how she had become a distraction. She was beautiful. I had watched her for months thinking she was nothing more than a stripper turned escort. And she had played her part well, she knew how to use her sexuality and had used it well to break down my defenses. But it was nothing more than acting. The woman I saw before me wasn't Michelle, even though I thought I could somehow see pieces of her.

"Here's your immunity agreement." She placed papers in front of me and grabbed the clear plastic bag that held my phone. "This better be good. I've pulled a hell of a lot of strings to get this done." She shoved her hand inside of the evidence bag and handed me my phone.

I took it from her and powered it on. While it powered on I started to read the agreement. She had come through. It granted me full immunity. I grabbed the pen she set out and signed it quickly. If she wanted a good story she was going to get a damn good story.

"You have it all wrong." She held her hand up to stop me from speaking.

"I need to record your statement." She pulled out a small camera and stand from her bag and set it up. "Continue."

"I don't know anything about Trent's involvement. You say he runs this organization or whatever but I honestly don't know what his role is, but the man that is calling the shots is Jacob, him and some other guy."

"How do you know this?"

"When I met Trent, Jacob blackmailed me and told me he would expose me if I didn't sleep with him." I lied. Well, it wasn't a complete lie. "He found out my history with Redd and basically sent for them."

"Sent for them for what?" Michelle looked like she was getting annoyed.

"I refuse to continue sleeping with him

and that's when Redd and Queen showed up. Instead of outing me to Trent he used them. They found me because of him and when I went to confront him I saw this." I grabbed my phone and accessed my iCloud drive. I found the video I had managed to keep for years and hit play.

The phone screen lit up with video of Jacob in the garage torturing and then ordering the killing of a man. I watched her as she watched in confusion.

"Why are the accounts in your name?"

"They set me up. Jacob knew my alias was fake and hoped they could never be traced to me. He convinced Trent it would be best to make someone not affiliated with the firm as a manager on the account."

I grabbed my phone and showed her the documents that Trent had. I had decided to keep him out of this. I would deal with him. I flipped through my phone and showed her the documents I had photographed, including the identification with Queen's face.

"When Redd showed up demanding his money back I did the one thing I knew how to do to make money, and that's sex. I thought I could help him make his money and go on with my life, but they had other plans." I am really hoping she believed this shit.

"Who's the other man in the video?"

"I don't know. I only know Jacob. He's threatened me, you have him ordering a killing and he was there the night you arrested all of us. He's the head I know it."

"We know he's involved." Michelle paused the recording before continuing. "You will have to testify and until you do you will be in WITSEC."

"Witsec?"

"Witness Protection."

"And how long will that take."

"As long as it takes. Within a few weeks you will be moved and given a different identity. Nothing new to you though." She rolled her eyes and began to pack her things. As she did, I scrolled through my phone and found Berto's number and hit erase.

"I'll take that." Michelle reached and grabbed my phone from my hands. "It's evidence."

I knew that was coming. I recited Berto's number over and over again, he should have been done with my stuff.

"So what happens to my accounts, my house, why can't I go home?"

"Because if you do nine times out of ten

you'll be killed. I don't think you realized you've been dancing with the devil all these years. We can't find Trent, and we know he's involved somehow no matter what you say. All assets will be frozen. I want you to understand. You won't be Kyra, you won't be Dominique, you can't go back."

Michelle stopped packing up her things and walked towards me. "It wasn't all fake Dominique." She leaned in and planted her lips against mine and kissed me. What kind of head game was this girl playing? "I worked hard to protect you. This will be your second chance, don't fuck it up.... Goodbye."

Michelle left and I was alone. Well, not completely alone there were those guys outside. I paced the floor back and forth. Things were just not going according to plan but I was going to get out of this. I be damn if I someone else decided what type of life I lived. I looked out the window. I was getting dark outside.

The men did hourly checks. I glanced at the clock on the wall. I had forty-five minutes before the next time. I grabbed my shoes and headed towards the back door, peaking out before leaving to make sure no officers were in the back.

I opened the door and then and dashed across the yard faster than Usain Bolt. I reached the fence and threw my shoes over into the next yard before pulling myself over. I repeated it over and over before I made it to a street. I never planned on testifying shit but I had to give them something that could keep me out of prison. There was no way I was escaping from behind bars.

I moved through the dark streets until I found a convenience store. I didn't know what area I was in but I was about to get the fuck out of here. I strolled in looking as normal as I possibly could, given the circumstances. I walked to the counter.

"You got a phone I can use?"

The clerk looked at me as if I was foreign. "Yeah." He breathed and handed me the cordless device. I quickly keyed in the number I had committed to memory. He answered on the first ring.

"I need a favor, there is another grand in it for you." This would be the most expensive ride I ever took. "Yeah, send someone to pick me up at this address. And hurry." I gave him the address and disconnected the call. I looked at the clerk.

"If someone comes looking for me I'm not here." I walked towards the restroom. I didn't know if the clerk would cover for me or not so I needed them to hurry. I ducked my head out the restroom to see there was anyone out here. A black Escalade slowly turned into the parking lot. The car window rolled down and I recognized the guy driving as one of the guys from Berto's spot.

I ran towards the car and jumped in, thankful that he had come through and not just forgot about me and stole my money. I rested my head against the headrest as we drove away. I couldn't wait to get my shit and get the hell out of Texas.

# CHAPTER 23

I stood on the balcony of my new beachfront condo. The Miami breeze washed across my skin. Three months later and I still couldn't believe that I had gotten away with that shit. As soon as I reached Berto's, I boarded a plan with my new identity and my millions.

"Hey Baby." That voice could always get my attention. His steamy baritone lulled me back into the present.

"It's about time you get here." I turned to face him and wrapped my arms around him. "I missed being in your arms." Trent kissed me deeply. It had been months since I felt this man. I pushed back to look at him.

"I missed you too Kyra. I just had to make sure my dad got out of the country before coming here. Are you sure there is no way he could be identified on the video you gave the Feds?"

"It's Amani now." I laughed before continuing. "His face was never visible in the video. But the bigger question is what happened? Why you go off script? We had a plan babe."

I had been dying to ask him this question.

"We were only supposed to frame them and Jacob. No one was supposed to die that night."

The night Trent walked in the house and told me I didn't know who he truly was I knew this man was down for me. Our house had been under surveillance for months and Jacob had become more and more disrespectful.

For years he had been skimming off the top, thinking he was calling the shots, so we had to dead that shit. And when Redd showed up I saw t as a perfect opportunity to be done with both of our threats. Being honest Redd had me going just a bit, a little caught up in those old feelings but nothing could ever come between Trent and I. We were one and the same. He was me and I was him.

"Yeah and there also wasn't supposed to be any Feds until I called in the tip. But desperate times babe, that nigga had been fucking my wife and stealing my money, he didn't deserve to live and Jacob bitch ass should have been laying next to him but someone needed to take the fall for that shit."

"Redd didn't know what he was walking into when he came back but none of that matters baby we good."

"Are we? What about the cop?"

"What about her? She was a wildcard, I had

no idea I was even on her radar. I don't know how she made me, but it's been dealt with. I think I gave her enough on Jacob to keep her busy."

Trent kissed me again. Every time our lips touched he gave me that feeling. Somehow all the things we had been through rekindled the fire. Every time he touched me I felt butterflies. I knew this man loved me unconditionally. He had accepted my flaws and I had accepted his. He had proven that he was gonna be my rider for life.

"You talk to your connect here?"

"Yeah, we gone be back on top in no time." He wrapped his arms around me as we watched the waves crash against the beach. As soon as I got to Miami I found us our own little piece of paradise and I knew he would find his way back to me. No matter what happened we always agreed to meet in Miami. Our escape plan didn't go as we planned but we always knew we would find each other again.

"We will run these streets baby, but this time no secrets okay." My head fell back against his shoulders and I exhaled. "This time around, full disclosure."

## ABOUT THE AUTHOR - DEIIRA SMITH-COLLARD

Deilra Smith-Collard is an author from Houston, Texas. With a creative writing style that intertwines fact with fiction, love and lust, and moral dilemmas, her books are thought to challenge the mind and question the lines of relationships, love and life.

Deilra's first novel, Love Lust & a Whole Lotta Distrust was self-published in 2008 and met with great reviews. After the success of the first novel, Deilra went on to write for Anexander Books, publishing her next 2 full length novels, Secrets, Sins and Shameful Lies and Role Play. In addition to her full length novels, she has also published a short story, My Extra and was also featured in 3 anthologies, Bedtime Stories ,Coffee Confessions and Love Never Fails.

In addition to writing Deilra Smith-Collard is also the Founder and Editor-In-Chief for Le Charme Magazine and a freelance photographer/graphic and web designer.

*Text **GETLIT** to **66866** for updates, giveaways and more!*

www.deiirasmithcollard.com

  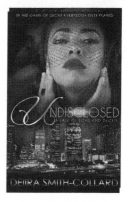

Made in the USA
Lexington, KY
17 May 2019